Olode the Hunter

by the same author

Folk Tales
The Piece of Fire and Other Haitian Tales
The King's Drum and Other African Stories
The Tiger's Whisker and Other Tales and Legends from Asia
  and the Pacific
The Hat-Shaking Dance and Other Tales from Ghana
Terrapin's Pot of Sense
Ride With the Sun
Kantchil's Lime Pit and Other Stories from Indonesia
The Cow-Tail Switch and Other West African Stories
  (with George Herzog)
The Fire on the Mountain and Other Ethiopian Stories
  (with Wolf Leslau)
Uncle Bouqui of Haiti

Novels
The African
The Big Old World of Richard Creeks
The Caballero

Non-Fiction
The Drum and the Hoe: Life and Lore of the Haitian People
Negro Folk Music U.S.A.
Haiti Singing
Negro Songs from Alabama
On Recognizing the Human Species
Vodoun in Haitian Culture
Shaping Our Times: What the United Nations Is and Does

by Harold Courlander

with Ezekiel A. Eshugbayi

Illustrated by Enrico Arno

OLODE
THE HUNTER
and
Other Tales
from Nigeria

Harcourt, Brace & World, Inc., New York

Contents

Ijapa ni o yo!
Omo re ni on bo!
Ijapa ni kini o bo?
Omo re ni kini o so wipe o yo?

Ijapa (the tortoise) said: "It emerges!"
His son cried out: "I seize it!"
Ijapa asked: "What did you seize?"
His son asked: "What did you say had emerged?"
—YORUBA PROVERB

Olomu's Bush Rat

HERE was a chief. His name was Olomu. In memory of him there is a saying:

> "The smell of the bush rat
> Is stronger than words."

It is said that once Olomu was traveling from one town to another. He was hungry, because in the night hyenas had come and eaten his food. Olomu's friends and servants went into the bush to find game. While he waited, he moved this way and that, and he came upon a trap in which a bush rat had been caught. He took the bush rat from the trap, thinking how good it would taste. He did not notice a poor country man, the owner of the trap, standing nearby. Olomu returned to his camp. He heard his servants and friends coming back. He was ashamed to be seen with game taken from a trap belonging to another man, and he quickly hid the bush rat under his cap. The servants brought meat. They prepared it for the chief. He ate.

Olomu continued his journey. The poor man from whose

trap the bush rat had been taken came also. He walked behind Olomu's party singing this song:

"Life is hard.
  Poverty oppresses me.
  Now a new disaster comes.
  I found one cowry.
  I spent it to buy a trap.
  My trap caught a bush rat.
  Olomu came and removed my bush rat.
  Olomu is a thief."

Olomu's servants and followers were surprised. They became angry. They threatened the country man. But he would not remain quiet. Olomu did not look to the left or the right. He was ashamed. The country man followed him, singing the song over and over again. When they passed people on the road, he sang more loudly so that they

would hear. Olomu, his servants, and his followers arrived at the town. The country man was still singing. When he was scolded by Olomu's soldiers, he paid no attention. When they threatened to beat him, he paid no attention. He went on singing. The town was in an uproar. Everyone was talking about the matter. The underchiefs came together. They said: "This country fellow is trying to ruin the chief's reputation. He should be punished." Others said: "It is so. But he has made an accusation. It must be looked into." So they went to the country man, saying: "We have heard what you are saying. Remain quiet now. We will look into it. There will be justice. If what you say is true, it shall fall on Olomu. If it is false, it shall fall on you. The words you have said are grave. If you lie, you shall be beaten and thrown into the bush."

So at last the country man was silent. He waited. But in the town other people began to sing the song he had composed. The underchiefs ordered guards to watch Olomu wherever he went, so that the bush rat might be found. When Olomu entered his house to sleep, the guards came with him. He did not know what to do with the bush rat. He left it where it was, on his head, and he slept with his cap on. In the morning he arose and went out. He felt the meat grow warm. Soon he could even smell it. He could not take a breath without smelling the bush rat.

Seven days went by. The underchiefs called a council, and they sent for Olomu. He came. He sat down in his place.

They questioned him. He said: "I am Olomu, the chief. Who dares say that I am a thief? Whoever says it, he is a scoundrel. Perhaps he is mad. Whenever has a paramount chief stolen? And whenever has he taken such a thing as a bush rat?" As he talked, the smell of decaying meat spread through the council. The underchiefs stopped asking questions. They stopped listening to Olomu. At last they ordered the guards to search him. One of the guards removed Olomu's cap. There, on top of Olomu's bald head, was the dead bush rat.

Olomu was ashamed. He got up; he walked away into the bush. He did not return, for the disgrace was too great. The country man was sent for. When he arrived, they paid him from what was in Olomu's house for the loss of his bush rat. They selected a new paramount chief. What happened was not forgotten, for people everywhere knew the song the country man had sung. And there came to be a saying:

"The smell of the bush rat
Is stronger than words."

The Man Who
Looked for Death

AIYE-GBEGE had everything. He was rich, for he had inherited great wealth from his father. He had land, gold, fine clothes, servants, and several wives. People admired and envied him. But it is said that a man who has never wanted for things does not know how to live with good fortune. This is the way it was with Aiye-Gbege. In all his life he had never had to work or earn money to live. He spent his money lavishly. A time came when it was gone. He sold his gold ornaments to buy food. Then he sold his land. Hard times came upon him. His servants left him. His wives went away, returning to the villages from which they had come. Aiye-Gbege was alone. He owned nothing. He asked for help from those he had befriended when he was rich, but now that Aiye-Gbege had nothing to give them, they ignored him. He begged for money in the streets. He suffered greatly. He decided to die.

He left the town and went out in search of Death. He went everywhere, but he could not find Death. He

15

went from one place to another, saying, "Is Death here?" But Death was not there. If he met a stranger on the trail he asked: "Have you seen Death?" Always the answer was the same: "One does not see Death until Death comes for him. It is Death who seeks."

But one day, meeting an old man on the trail, he asked the usual questions. The old man said: "Death cannot be found easily. But you can speak to his agent, Ayo. You will find him in such and such a place."

Aiye-Gbege went on. He found Ayo. He told him the story of his miseries. "I inherited great wealth from my father. I was rich. Then hard times came upon me. My wealth is gone, my wives and servants have left me. I have nothing. I suffer. Therefore, I seek Death. I cannot find him. For this reason I came to you, who are his agent."

Ayo answered: "I will arrange it. I will see to it for you. But you will have to wait a little. Be patient. Meanwhile, so that your sufferings are not too great to bear, I will help you." Ayo called his servants. They took Aiye-Gbege and bathed him. They put fine clothes on him and hung gold ornaments around his neck. They fed him. And before Aiye-Gbege left the place, Ayo gave him a sack of money and a horse to carry him home.

Aiye-Gbege was astounded at what had happened. When he arrived at his town, word went out. People came and paid him their respects. His servants returned and went to work. His wives heard and returned from their villages. Life went on. The money Ayo had given him seemed endless. Aiye-Gbege lived more lavishly than he had lived before. He was happy. When a year had passed, he decided to have a great gathering to celebrate the anniversary of his good fortune. He sent word everywhere inviting people to come. On the day of the festival the town was crowded. There was dancing, and the sound of drums and gongs filled the air. Aiye-Gbege gave presents of money to everyone. The people praised him in songs. He drank much palm wine. He felt the goodness of everything, and because of this, he went into the middle of things and began to dance. The people stood back, watching him and praising him. Aiye-Gbege then decided to show his skill as a horseman. He climbed on his most spirited horse and made him dance. He raced his horse back and forth. Because Aiye-Gbege had drunk much palm wine he tried to do even greater things. He stood up and tried to dance on his horse's back. But the wine was too much for him. He

slipped from the horse and fell upon the hard ground. He lay as though dead, his eyes closed. Seeing this, the people at the celebration turned and went away. The drumming stopped. There was silence.

Aiye-Gbege opened his eyes. Standing before him was Death. Death said: "As it was arranged with Ayo, my agent, I have come for you."

Aiye-Gbege said: "No, I do not want you. Go away."

Death said: "You, Aiye-Gbege, you looked for me everywhere. You asked for me to come."

Aiye-Gbege said: "That was when I had nothing in the world. Now I have everything. I do not need you. I am happy."

Death answered: "In hardship, when you had nothing, you lived. Too much happiness has killed you."

Death took Aiye-Gbege.

Before those times it had been said that people died of three things—war, famine, and sickness. But after the time of Aiye-Gbege a fourth thing was added, and there came to be a saying that people died in war, in famine, in sickness, and in happiness.

Ekun and Opolo Go
Looking for Wives

EKUN the leopard was looking for a wife. In his own village there was not a single family that wanted him as a son-in-law, for he had a bad reputation. He was not trusted. One day Ekun went to Opolo the frog, saying, "I have received a message from a distant place. There is a chief there. He wants me to become his son-in-law. He has two daughters. Therefore, let us go together. You too can be his son-in-law."

Opolo the frog replied: "Has the chief ever heard of me? Why should he give me one of his daughters?"

Ekun said: "The chief respects me. I will speak for you. I will vouch for your character and your family."

Opolo said: "Yes, very well, I will go with you."

They prepared for the journey. Opolo bathed and put on his best clothes. Ekun had only the ragged clothes he wore. They set out. When they passed people on the road, there were comments about Opolo: "What a fine personage! See how well he is dressed! Look at his dignity!" Sometimes it was said: "How easy it is to see who

19

is the master and who is the servant! One carries himself with pride; the other shuffles miserably." Opolo did not notice these things, but Ekun heard. He thought about the matter.

At last he said: "We are two friends. We drink from the same gourd. Let us share our clothes also. Tomorrow you can wear my clothes, and I shall wear yours. The next day we shall change again. Thus two friends become close."

Opolo agreed. The next morning they changed clothes. As they walked along the trail, people said: "See who is the master and who is the servant. Ekun, there, he is rich and handsome, while Opolo is careless of his looks."

Every morning they changed. It went on this way. When they arrived at the outskirts of the chief's town, Opolo said: "Ekun, we have arrived. Now give me my own clothes to wear. I will give you yours."

But Ekun had no such intention. Before the frog could say another word, Ekun leaped upon him and swallowed him.

He entered the town. People admired his appearance. Word came to the chief. He sent for Ekun. He asked him: "Where is your village? Why are you here?"

Ekun said: "Sir, I have made a long journey in search of a wife. Your daughters, I have heard of them. Therefore, I came."

The chief said: "You make a good appearance. But giving a daughter is an important thing. Let us wait a little. Let us become acquainted. We shall ponder it."

"Yes," Ekun said, "that is the right way."

20

But now Opolo spoke from Ekun's belly. He said: "The chief, he is stupid."

The chief heard. He said to Ekun: "What did I hear?"

Ekun answered: "Oh, great chief, that was merely my belly making sounds. It was not I who spoke."

As Ekun went through the chief's gate, Opolo spoke from inside, saying, "Ah, how well I cheat the chief!"

The chief's guards were angry. They said: "You, whoever you are, no one cheats the chief!"

Ekun said: "It was not I who said such a thing! It was merely my belly making sounds!"

He went out. He walked through the market. People looked at him in admiration. But Opolo spoke from inside, saying: "The chief's daughters, they are ugly."

Ekun protested: "The sounds, they are not mine." But word was carried to the chief that Ekun had insulted his daughters.

The chief sent for him. He said: "You, Ekun, though I have received you in my house, it is said you have insulted my daughters."

Ekun said: "How could it be? For I wish to be your son-in-law."

Opolo added, from inside: ". . . even though you are considered the worst of all chiefs."

The chief heard. He frowned. Ekun said quickly: "Sir, the sounds you heard were not my words, they were merely rumblings in my belly!"

Ekun went away from the chief's house. The chief said: "This person Ekun, he has a remarkable belly."

As Ekun passed a group of elderly men at the chief's

gate, he spoke respectfully. But his belly called out: "Your bald heads resemble eggs in a nest." The men were angered.

But Ekun said: "Oh, it is my belly again! Do not listen to what it says!"

Ekun's belly would not remain still. Everywhere he went it was making sounds that insulted people.

One day word came that an enemy army was approaching the town. The chief's warriors assembled with their weapons. The chief said: "Where is Ekun, he who wants to be my son-in-law?"

Messengers went to find Ekun. They found him and said: "Take up your weapons. The enemy are attacking."

Ekun did not wish to fight. He said: "I would come, but there is a lameness in my back."

Opolo added in a loud voice from inside: "Nevertheless, I will come."

"That is good," the messengers said.

Ekun said: "Unfortunately, I did not bring any weapons . . ."

Opolo added: "Yet I am sure the chief will provide me."

The messengers said: "Yes, come at once. Our chief will give you weapons."

Ekun went with them to where the chief's warriors were assembled. He was afraid. He pointed in a certain direction, saying, "Let us go there. That is where the enemy are." But his belly spoke, saying, "No, that is not really the right direction. Let us go the other way."

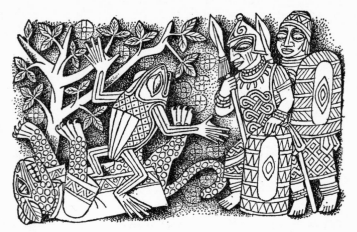

They went the other way. They met the enemy. They fought. But Ekun hid in the bush. Some of the chief's warriors called out: "Ekun, Ekun, where are you?"

Ekun did not answer. He wanted to remain hidden. But Opolo answered from his belly, saying, "Here! I am here!" He repeated it over and over. "Here! I am here!" The enemy warriors heard. They came to where Ekun was hiding. They killed him. Then they ran away because the chief's warriors were winning the battle.

The chief's warriors found Ekun's body. Opolo the frog came out. He reclaimed the clothes that were his. He put them on. He returned to the town with the men. The chief received him. He gave Opolo one of his daughters to marry, and Opolo became his son-in-law. The frog returned to his village. Ekun the leopard never returned. His greed and his bad character overcame him. So it is said.

The Lizard's Lost Meat

FEMALE hyena was on her way to a distant market to procure some food. She arrived at a place where a large crowd had gathered. Drums were beating. She went into the crowd and asked: "What is happening here? Why is there so much excitement? Why is there drumming?"

Someone replied: "It is a wrestling contest."

She asked: "Who is wrestling?"

They said: "Whoever chooses to wrestle, he wrestles."

She went forward. She saw the wrestlers. They were a bush rat and a frog. The wrestlers grasped each other. They pushed. They pulled. Neither one had the advantage. But at last the bush rat threw the frog down. The frog was finished. The bush rat picked him up and carried him away.

The female hyena said: "Where does the bush rat take the frog?"

They answered: "He who wins the contest gets the loser for his meat. That is the way it is done. The bush rat

24

contested with the frog. He won. Therefore, the frog becomes the meat of the bush rat."

The leopard came out of the crowd. He said: "I challenge the goat."

The goat answered: "How would it serve me to wrestle with you? I don't eat meat. If I throw you, what can I do with you?"

The leopard answered: "Why do you stand back afraid?"

The goat said: "What purpose is in it? I eat only grass."

The leopard said: "Can you wrestle with the grass? Come forward then. Tighten your waistcloth. Let us begin."

So they wrestled. Each took hold of the other. They strained. They struggled. The leopard threw the goat. He picked him up. He carried him off.

The lion came forward. He challenged the deer. They wrestled. The lion won and carried his meat away.

The female hyena spoke. She said: "I challenge the antelope."

People murmured. They said: "When has a woman ever wrestled? This is only for men. Take yourself to the market."

But the female hyena refused to leave. "It has never been said that a woman may not wrestle. I wish to wrestle the antelope."

They said to the antelope: "A woman has challenged you."

The antelope said: "There is a proverb. It says, 'If a

25

woman will not cook fufu, send her with a spear to hunt.' Since this woman will not go to market, let her wrestle." So the antelope came forward and wrestled with the hyena. The hyena was strong. She threw the antelope. She picked him up and carried him home.

The male hyena was surprised. He said: "Where did you find this meat?"

His wife answered: "There is a wrestling match going on in the bush. Whoever wins takes the meat of the loser. I wrestled with the antelope. I defeated him."

The male hyena said: "If a woman can win an antelope, how much more can a man win?"

He went into the bush. He found the wrestling match. He looked around. His eyes fell on the lizard. He said: "What is that one's name?"

The lizard said: "I am called No-Room-for-Both."

The hyena said: "Good. Let us wrestle."

The lizard came to the center. He tightened his waistcloth. The hyena tightened his waistcloth. They met. They struggled. Dust rose in the air. Their feet packed down the earth. The hyena became tired. The lizard threw him down. The crowd applauded. The lizard spoke, saying, "Lend me a knife that I may cut my meat into parts. That way I can carry it." The hyena became frightened. He struggled to his feet. He ran into the bush. He escaped.

The hyena returned home bruised and bleeding. His wife said: "Did you wrestle? Where is the meat?"

He answered: "I fought a fierce creature. He was too

large. He cast a shadow larger than a house. Therefore, he won. So I went away quickly."

His wife said: "What is the name of this terrible creature?"

He replied: "I do not know. They referred to him as No-Room-for-Both."

His wife said: "I have never heard of this creature."

Thereafter, whenever an animal passed on the trail, the female hyena would ask her husband: "Is it he?"

And the hyena would say: "No, that is the leopard," or, "That is the vulture," or whatever the animal was called in the bush. But the lizard had not given up looking for his lost meat. He came to the hyena's house one day. He crawled up the house post by the door. No one noticed him, so he said: "Crik."

They looked. The hyena's wife said: "It is the lizard." But the hyena leaped up. He shouted: "It is he! It is

No-Room-for-Both! If he lives here, I must go else-where!" He ran from the house. His wife followed him. They went deep into the bush. They did not return but remained there forever. That is why the lizard is often seen in the village, but the hyena no longer lives there.

The Antelope Skin

ONCE there lived a hunter named Olaiya. He was a hunter of skill. He rarely went into the bush without returning with meat. There came a time when game was scarce. Many hunters went into the bush to find game, but they returned with nothing. Olaiya said to them: "A good hunter goes into the bush with his gun. He finds game. He pursues it. He kills it. He returns with meat. What kind of hunters are you? You go into the bush, you come home with nothing."

The other hunters were angered by Olaiya's words. They said: "Talk is not food."

Olaiya said: "Tomorrow I will hunt. I will find game. I will kill it. I will return with meat. This is the way it is with a true hunter."

Early the next morning, while the sky was still dark, Olaiya arose. He took his gun. He fastened his gourd of powder to his belt. He took his skinning knife. He departed from the village.

He walked far, looking for a sign of game, but he

29

found none. Olaiya went everywhere he had ever hunted, but he found nothing, not even a bush rat. So he went beyond, deep into the forest. Still he found nothing. Night came. He lay down and slept. When day came again, he continued hunting. At last, in a clearing, he saw an antelope. He approached silently, put powder in his gun and fired. The antelope fell.

Olaiya was delighted. He put down his gun and began to skin the antelope. When he was finished, he put the skin aside. He sat down to rest, thinking, "This is the way it is with a true hunter. He does not give up. He can be depended upon."

Suddenly the antelope sprang to its feet. Olaiya said: "You, antelope, you can't go away without your skin!"

The antelope said: "You, hunter, this forest is my home. You have taken my skin, but that is all."

Olaiya said: "You, antelope, stand where you are! Your friends will laugh if they see you without skin!"

The antelope replied: "You, hunter, your friends will laugh when they see you without meat." And he ran among the big trees and was lost. Olaiya followed with his gun, but he could not find the antelope.

At last he went back to the clearing. He took the skin and returned to his village. The people gathered around him, saying: "Olaiya, where is the meat?"

Olaiya said: "I went into the forest. I found an antelope. I killed him. I took this skin from him. Before I had a chance to cut up the meat, the antelope arose and departed."

30

Olaiya's story was greeted with laughter. People said: "He went hunting for meat. He came back with an antelope skin. What kind of hunter is this?"

Olaiya said: "I told the story truly. Here is the skin to prove it."

They went away from him, shaking their heads. They said: "Who ever heard of a skinned antelope running away?"

As for Olaiya, he told his story again and again, holding up the antelope skin as proof. But it was no use.

And there came to be a saying in the village:

> "Displaying an antelope hide
> Quiets no one's hunger."

Olode the Hunter
Becomes an Oba

HERE was a hunter in the land. Bad luck dogged him. He had nothing in the world except the hut he lived in on the edge of the village, his gun, and a single cloth to wrap around his loins. He was so poor that he had never been able to take a wife. His relatives, some had gone away; some had died. He was alone. In the village, people did not even acknowledge that he had a name. They merely called him Olode, meaning hunter.

Olode went hunting one day. He followed the tracks of the game, but he caught nothing. He went deeper and deeper into the forest. He went farther than he had ever gone before. Because the trees were large and the foliage dense, it was dark. Olode struggled through the thick underbrush and waded through swamps. He found no game. He was discouraged. He sat down to rest. He closed his eyes for a moment. When he opened them, he saw a fierce-looking manlike creature standing before him. He sprang to his feet. But the creature said: "Put away the gun. I am Oluigbo, King of the Bush."

Olode put his gun away. Oluigbo said: "You, man, what brings you here?"

Olode said: "I am a hunter. I followed the game tracks. There was no game to be found. I am hungry. I must find meat. I must have skins to sell. Therefore, I pressed into the bush. I arrived at this place."

Oluigbo said: "Indeed, you are poor. It meets the eye."

They talked. They smoked together. Olode spoke of his misery. "I am alone. I have no son. I have no wife. My family, they are scattered and gone. Good fortune, it eludes me. I have no ointment for the sores on my legs. It is this way with me."

Oluigbo said: "Yes, it is visible. Say no more."

They smoked in silence. The King of the Bush arose at last. He put out the fire from his pipe. He said: "Hunter, to the most miserable person there must come at least one good thing. Therefore, follow me."

Olode arose. He followed Oluigbo to a great tree standing among smaller trees. Oluigbo said: "Throw down the gun." Olode threw it down. Oluigbo said: "Throw down your loincloth." Olode threw it down. Then Oluigbo struck the great tree with his hand. A door opened. "Enter," Oluigbo said. Olode entered. The door closed. Olode found himself at the gate of a large town. People were waiting for him. They welcomed him with dancing and hand-clapping. They brought clothing for him and covered his naked body. They placed him in a carrying chair and carried him into the town. A servant held a large red parasol over his head to shield him from the sun. A drummer went ahead of the procession beating out signals that said: "The Oba, our king, has arrived."

They carried Olode to the king's compound. There was a wall, and inside were many houses. The procession stopped, and the elders of the town came and touched their foreheads in the dust. One of them, the oldest, said: "Olode, we receive you as our new Oba. The town and the land around it are yours. You are our father. You will dispense justice. You will dispense charity. You will govern. All things that belong to an Oba are yours. Only one thing is forbidden."

To Olode it seemed like a dream. He said: "What is forbidden?"

The old man answered: "Inside the third house there is a carved door. The room behind it must never be entered. Do you accept the condition?"

"I accept," Olode said.

There was feasting, dancing, and music. An animal was sacrificed. Olode was proclaimed Oba. Messengers went out beating iron gongs to announce the event everywhere.

The days came, one after another. Olode did the things that a king is expected to do. He ruled. He dispensed charity. He collected taxes. He judged the lawsuits that were brought to him. He ate. Poverty fell away from him. He chose a wife. He had children. All was well with Olode.

But now that all was well, he remembered how it used to be, when he could not buy even a small gourd of palm wine. So he ordered that palm wine be brought. He drank much of it. When it was gone he called for more. He came to think only of palm wine. Instead of caring for the people, he drank. The days went on. Olode forgot everything but his drinking. When he walked he staggered from drunkenness.

And one day he entered the third house and stood in front of the carved door. He said: "Am I not the Oba? Who can forbid anything to a king? Is not the land mine? And everything in the land? Is not this house mine? Therefore, the door is mine. I will open it."

He pushed against the door. It opened. It was dark beyond. Olode stepped across the threshold. The door closed behind him. He looked back. There was nothing there, no house, no town. All around him there was nothing but forest. He saw that he was naked. On the ground at his feet were his gun and his old ragged loincloth. He put the ragged cloth around him. He searched for the town. It was not there.

So it was that Olode the hunter found good fortune and lost it.

There is a saying among the people:

"The hunting dog must listen to the hunter's horn,
Otherwise the forest will devour him."

Thus it was with Olode. He did not listen. He accepted the condition when he became king. Then in drunkenness he went through the forbidden door. The forest devoured him.

How Ijapa,
Who Was Short,
Became Long

IJAPA the tortoise was on a journey. He was tired and hungry, for he had been walking a long time. He came to the village where Ojola the boa lived, and he stopped there, thinking, "Ojola will surely feed me, for I am famished."

Ijapa went to Ojola's house. Ojola greeted him, saying, "Enter my house and cool yourself in the shade, for I can see you have been on the trail."

Ijapa entered. They sat and talked. Ijapa smelled food cooking over the fire. He groaned with hunger, for when Ijapa was hungry he was more hungry than anyone else. Ojola said politely: "Surely the smell of my food does not cause you pain?"

Ijapa said: "Surely not, my friend. It only made me think that if I were at home now, my wife would be cooking likewise."

Ojola said: "Let us prepare ourselves. Then we shall eat together."

Ijapa went outside. He washed himself in a bowl of

water. When he came in again he saw the food in the
middle of the room and smelled its odors. But Ojola the
boa was coiled around the food. There was no way to
get to it. Ijapa walked around and around, trying to
find an opening through which he could approach the
waiting meal. But Ojola's body was long, and his coils
lay one atop the other, and there was no entrance through
them. Ijapa's hunger was intense.

Ojola said: "Come, do not be restless. Sit down. Let
us eat."

Ijapa said: "I would be glad to sit with you. But you,
why do you surround the dinner?"

Ojola said: "This is our custom. When my people
eat, they always sit this way. Do not hesitate any longer."
The boa went on eating while Ijapa again went around
and around trying to find a way to the food. At last
he gave up. Ojola finished eating. He said: "What a
pleasure it is to eat dinner with a friend."

Ijapa left Ojola's house hungrier than he had come. He returned to his own village. There he ate. He brooded on his experience with Ojola. He decided that he would return the courtesy by inviting Ojola to his house to eat with him. He told his wife to prepare a meal for a certain festival day. And he began to weave a long tail out of grass. He spent many days weaving the tail. When it was finished, he fastened it to himself with tree gum.

On the festival day, Ojola arrived. They greeted each other at the door, Ijapa saying, "You have been on a long journey. You are hungry. You are tired. Refresh yourself at the spring. Then we shall eat."

Ojola was glad. He went to the spring to wash. When he returned, he found Ijapa already eating. Ijapa's grass tail was coiled several times around the food. Ojola could not get close to the dinner. Ijapa ate with enthusiasm. He stopped sometimes to say: "Do not hesitate, friend Ojola. Do not be shy. Good food does not last forever."

Ojola went around and around. It was useless. At last he said: "Ijapa, how did it happen that once you were quite short but now you are very long?"

Ijapa said: "One person learns from another about such things." Ojola then remembered the time Ijapa had been his guest. He was ashamed. He went away. It was from Ijapa that came the proverb:

"The lesson that a man should be short came
    from his fellow man.
The lesson that a man should be tall also came
    from his fellow man."

Ijapa Cries
for His Horse

IT happened one time that Ijapa the tortoise owned a fine white horse with beautiful trappings. When Ijapa sat on his horse, he felt proud and vain because he was the center of all eyes. Instead of working his garden, he rode from place to place so that everyone could see him. If he came to a town on market day, he rode his horse through the crowded market so that he might hear people say: "What a distinguished stranger! What an important person!" If he came to a village in the evening, he rode before the headman's house so that his presence would be properly noted. And because Ijapa appeared so distinguished on his white horse, the headman would provide him with food and a place to sleep and then send him on his way with dignity. Never had life been so good for Ijapa.

One day Ijapa arrived at the city of Wasimi. As he rode through the streets, he attracted great attention. People said: "He appears to be an important merchant," or, "He looks like a hero returning from battle." Word went to the

compound of the Oba, or king, that an important personage had arrived. When Ijapa appeared at the Oba's palace, he was welcomed with courtesy and dignity. The Oba's family took him to the guest house and brought him food. When night fell and it was time to sleep, they said: "We shall take care of the horse."

But Ijapa said: "Oh, no, I will keep him here with me in the guest house."

People said: "A horse has never before slept in the guest house."

Ijapa said: "My horse and I are like brothers. Therefore he always shares my sleeping quarters." So the horse was left in the guest house with Ijapa, and the Oba's household slept.

In the middle of the night, Ijapa heard his horse groan. He arose, lighted a torch, and went to see what was the matter. His horse was dead.

Ijapa cried out: "My horse! My horse!" Ijapa's cries

awakened everyone. The Oba's servants came. They tried to console Ijapa and quiet him. But he would not be consoled. He kept crying out: "My horse! My fine white horse! He is dead! He is dead!"

Members of the Oba's family came. They said: "Do not cry out so. In their time, all horses die. Be consoled."

But Ijapa went on mourning the death of his horse in a loud voice that was heard everywhere. At last the Oba himself came to the guest house. He listened to Ijapa's cries, and he said: "Do not cry any more. To soothe your misery, I will give you one of my own horses."

One of the Oba's best horses was brought into the guest house. Ijapa stopped crying. He thanked the Oba. People went back to their beds. Once more, the night was quiet. Ijapa kept the torch burning so that he could see his new horse. Then, suddenly, he began to cry again: "Oh, misfortune! Oh, how awful it is! See how I am suffering! Who has brought this terrible thing to happen!"

The servants came back. The Oba's family came back. They couldn't quiet Ijapa. Then the Oba appeared. He said: "Why do you continue this way? Your lost horse has been replaced."

Ijapa said: "Sir, I cannot help crying out when I think of my bad fortune. The horse you gave me is a fine one. So was my own white horse that died. If he had not died, how lucky I would have been, for I now would have two fine horses instead of one." And again Ijapa broke into loud cries: "Oh, misery! Oh, misfortune! How awful it is!"

They could not stop him. So the Oba said: "Very well,

if it is only your need for two horses that keeps the city awake, think no more about it. I will give you another horse." The servants brought another horse. Ijapa stopped crying. He thanked the Oba for his kindness. Everyone went back to bed. They slept. Only Ijapa couldn't sleep. He kept thinking about his good fortune. He had come with one horse. Now he had two.

Then his eyes fell upon the dead horse. He began to cry: "Oh, great misfortune! Oh, terrible thing! How awful it is! Bad luck falls on my head! Oh, misery!" He went on crying.

Again the household was awakened. Again they came and tried to console him. Again the Oba himself had to come. The Oba said: "This grief for a dead horse is too much. Many men have horses. Their horses die. But men cannot grieve forever."

Ijapa said: "Sir, I cannot help it. I looked at my dead white horse. I realized that only a few hours ago he was alive. Had he not died, I would own three fine horses and be the most fortunate of men!"

The Oba was tired. He was cross. But he ordered another horse be brought for Ijapa. "You are now the most fortunate of men," the Oba said. "You own three fine horses. Now let us all sleep." The family and the servants returned to their beds. They slept.

And then, just when everything had become quiet, Ijapa began crying out in grief again: "Oh, misery! Oh, misfortune! What a terrible thing has happened!" It went on and on. The Oba called his servants. He gave them instructions. They went to the guest house and took the

Oba's three horses away. They took Ijapa to the gate and pushed him out.

He had no horse at all now, and he went on foot like ordinary people. He returned to his own village in shame, for he had ridden away like a distinguished person and now his legs were covered with dust.

Kigbo and
the Bush Spirits

I n a certain village there was a young man named Kigbo. He had a character all his own. He was an obstinate person. If silence was pleasing to other people, he would play a drum. If someone said, "Tomorrow we should repair the storage houses," Kigbo said, "No, tomorrow we should sharpen our hoes." If his father said, "Kigbo, the yams are ripe. Let us bring them in," Kigbo said, "On the contrary, the yams are not ready." If someone said, "This is the way a thing should be done," Kigbo said, "No, it is clear that the thing should be done the other way around."

Kigbo married a girl of the village. Her name was Dolapo. He built a house of his own. His first child was a boy named Ojo. Once when the time came for preparing the fields, Kigbo's father said to him: "Let us go out tomorrow and clear new ground."

Kigbo said: "The fields around the village are too small. Let us go into the bush instead."

His father said: "No one farms in the bush."

Kigbo said: "Why does no one farm in the bush?"

His father said: "Men must have their fields near their houses."

Kigbo said: "I want to have my fields far from my house."

His father said: "It is dangerous to farm in the bush."

Kigbo replied: "The bush suits my taste."

Kigbo's father did not know what else to say. He called Kigbo's mother, saying, "He wants to farm in the bush. Reason with him."

Kigbo's mother said: "Do not go. The bush spirits will make trouble for you."

Kigbo said: "Ho! They will not trouble me. My name is Kigbo."

His father called for an elder of the village. The village elder said: "Our ancestors taught us to avoid the bush spirits."

Kigbo said: "Nevertheless, I am going."

He went to his house. His wife Dolapo stood at the door holding Ojo in her arms. Kigbo said: "Prepare things for me. Tomorrow I am going into the bush." In the morning he took his bush knife and his knapsack and walked a great distance. He found a place and said: "I will make my farm here."

He began to cut down the brush. At the sound of his chopping many bush spirits came out of the trees. They said: "Who is cutting here?"

Kigbo said: "It is I, Kigbo."

They said: "This land belongs to the bush spirits."

Kigbo said: "I do not care." He went on cutting.

The bush spirits said: "This is bush-spirit land. Therefore, we also will cut." They joined him in clearing the land. There were hundreds of them, and the cutting was soon done.

Kigbo said: "Now I will burn." He began to gather the brush and burn it.

The bush spirits said: "This is our land. Whatever you do, we will do it, too." They also gathered and burned brush. Soon it was done.

Kigbo returned to his village. He put corn seed in his knapsack. His father said: "Since you have returned, stay here. Do not go back to the bush."

His mother said: "Stay and work in the village. The bush is not for men."

Kigbo said: "In the bush no one gives me advice. The bush spirits help me." To his wife Dolapo he said: "Wait here in the village. I will plant. When the field is ready to be harvested, I will come for you."

He departed. When he arrived at his farm in the bush, he began to plant. The bush spirits came out of the trees. They said: "Who is there?"

He replied: "It is I, Kigbo. I am planting corn."

They said: "This land belongs to the bush spirits. Therefore, we also will plant. Whatever you do, we will do." They took corn seed from Kigbo's knapsack. They planted. Soon it was finished.

Kigbo went to a village where he had friends. He rested there, waiting for the corn to be grown. In his own village his wife, Dolapo, and his son, Ojo, also waited. Time passed. There was no message from Kigbo. At last Dolapo could wait no longer. She went into the bush to find her husband, carrying Ojo on her hip. They came to Kigbo's farm. The corn stalks were grown, but the corn was not yet ripe.

Ojo said: "I want some corn."

His mother said: "The corn is not yet ripe."

Ojo said: "I am hungry."

Dolapo broke off a stem of corn and gave it to him. The bush spirits came out of the trees, saying, "Who is there and what are you doing?"

She replied: "It is I, the wife of Kigbo. I broke off a stem of corn to give the little one."

They said: "Whatever you do, we will do." They swarmed through the field breaking off the corn stalks. Soon it was done, and all the broken stalks lay on the ground.

At this moment Kigbo arrived. He saw Dolapo and Ojo, and he saw all the corn lying on the ground. He said: "The corn is ruined!"

Dolapo said: "The bush spirits did it. I broke off only one stalk. It was Ojo's fault. He demanded a stalk to eat. I gave him a stalk, then the bush spirits did the rest." She gave Ojo a slap.

The bush spirits came out of the trees. They said: "What are you doing?"

Dolapo said: "I slapped the boy to punish him."

They said: "Whatever you do, we will do." They gathered around Ojo and began to slap him.

Kigbo shouted at his wife: "See what you have done!" In anger he slapped her.

The bush spirits said: "What are you doing?"

He said: "Slapping my wife for giving me so much trouble."

They said: "We will do it too." They stopped slapping the boy and began slapping Dolapo.

Kigbo called out for them to stop, but they wouldn't stop. He cried out: "Everything is lost!" He struck his head with his fist.

The bush spirits said: "What are you doing?"

He said: "All is lost. Therefore, I hit myself."

They said: "We will do it too." They gathered around Kigbo, striking him on the head.

He called out: "Let us go quickly!" Kigbo, Dolapo, and their son returned to the village, leaving the farm behind. He saw his father. Because of shame, Kigbo did not speak.

His father said: "Kigbo, let us go out with the men tomorrow and work in the fields."

Kigbo said: "Yes, Father, let us do so."

The Chief's Knife

N a certain village there was a chief. He owned a beautiful forged knife made by a celebrated iron-worker in the kingdom of Benin. Its designs were inlaid with copper and brass, and the chief valued it highly. There was a great dance in the village one time in the chief's honor. People came from everywhere. The chief gave out gifts. When the dancing was ended, the people went away. The next day the chief could not find his knife. He sent servants to look for it. They could not find it. He said at last: "My knife inlaid with copper and brass, it was given to me by my uncle. Yesterday I had it in my hand. Today it is gone. Someone has stolen it. Therefore, let the countryside be searched. He who has taken this thing, he will be punished."

People said: "Whoever could have had so much foolishness in him to let him steal a thing belonging to the chief?" Word was carried here and there that the knife must be found. Word came to the village of Gbo. The people looked around. Their eyes fell upon a young hunter. They said to him: "Were you not in the chief's village at the celebration?"

He said: "Yes, I was there. I ate, I danced."

They said: "Does not a hunter need a knife?"

He replied: "I have weapons already. I would not skin game with a knife belonging to a chief."

They said: "He answers too sharply. He is not respectful. His eyes are too angry. If he is innocent, why does he speak in this fashion?"

The hunter went away. People said: "Did you notice how he said just so much, then no more? He broke off speaking. He turned his back. He is surely the thief." The days came and the nights came. When the hunter went out of his house, they watched him. When he returned with his meat from the forest, they watched him. They began to comment. "See how suspiciously he

walks," one man said. "He has something to hide." Another said: "Yes, and he spends much time in the bush. What can he be doing there?" And yet another: "He speaks little. He avoids us. Surely he is the one who took the chief's knife."

Wherever he went, he was noticed. The days went by. And now when he spoke, people answered roughly, not wanting to be seen talking to the hunter. He had to take his leopard skins to another village to sell them, for in the village of Gbo no one would buy. It was clear to all that the hunter was not a good man. "See how he comes out of his house in the early dawn, before the village is awake," some said. "This is the mark of a man who has offended the community." "Yes, and notice how he returns to his house in the darkness, when his face can't be seen," others said. Someone suggested that the chief be told that the thief was in their village. Others said: "No, it would only bring shame on the village, and the chief would be hard on us." As for the hunter, he was alone, and now sometimes he stayed at night in the forest instead of coming home.

Then one day a messenger from the chief reported that the forged knife inlaid with brass and copper had been found. The chief himself had placed it in the rafters of his house, and it had fallen into the grass wall. The people of Gbo were pleased. They went about their affairs. When the hunter came out of his house in the early dawn, someone said: "See how hard the hunter works, how long his days are." When the hunter returned late at night, someone said: "See how determined he is. He will not return home without game." Someone greeted the hunter, and he answered with only a few words. "See how it is with him," someone said. "He does not talk too much like some people do. He is not vain like other hunters." When they saw him walking across the fields, they said: "See how he walks, afraid of nothing, full of courage." They admired the hunter in every way. They said: "One need only look at him to see that he is an honest man."

So it came to be said:

"When the chief's knife is stolen,
The hunter walks like a thief.
When the chief's knife is found,
The hunter is praised."

Why the Lion, the Vulture,
and the Hyena
Do Not Live Together

IT is said that once, for a brief time, Kiniun the lion, Igun the vulture, and Ikoko the hyena shared a house. This is the way it happened.

They met one day around the body of an antelope that the lion had killed. The vulture said: "We have many things in common. We eat the same kind of food. We should be companions. Therefore let us live in the same house."

They discussed the matter. They decided to live together. They built their house and went inside.

The hyena said: "This is a good thing we have done. But until now we have not sheltered under the same roof. We should know more about one another so that no one will give offense by accident. If a person knows what is offensive to another man, he may avoid trouble."

The lion and the vulture agreed. Because the lion was the eldest, they asked him to speak first.

"Above all," the lion said, "I wish to be respected. When a person is in my presence he should not stare in my face. It is contrary to good behavior."

"Yes, yes, it is so," the vulture and the hyena replied.

Then it was the hyena's turn. He was ashamed because his hind legs were shorter than his front legs, and he did not like other people to speak of it. "As for me," the hyena said, "what I object to most is having people talk about me when I am not present. All other things I can tolerate, but not this."

The lion and the vulture answered: "Yes, yes, it is so. One should not gossip about a person when he is not present."

It was the vulture's turn. He said: "I ask respect only for the crest of feathers on my head. It gives me a good appearance. When I appear, people say, 'See, there goes Igun. How well he dresses! Even his head is adorned with feathers.' Therefore, respect the feathers on my head."

"Yes, yes," the lion and the hyena said, "your crest will be respected."

They lived in the house together. They slept. In the morning the hyena arose and went out of the house. But he remained nearby and listened. When he was alone with the vulture, the lion said: "Why should the hyena object if people speak about him? It does not matter that his hind legs are short, because his fore legs are long. Would he not be far worse off if all his legs were short?"

The hyena heard. He re-entered the house filled with anger. But he feared the lion, so he said nothing. He merely looked the lion in the eyes as though to say: "Your words, I have heard them."

It was the lion's turn to become angry. He said: "You,

there, did we not discuss it last night? Was it not said that you should not stare in my face? It was agreed. And now you stare as though we had discussed nothing. It is not respectful."

The hyena said: "And was it not agreed that you would not speak of me behind my back? I went out only for a moment, and you began speaking of my legs."

They argued. They began to fight. As they struggled back and forth, they kicked up hot embers from the fire over which the vulture was cooking. A bit of the fire fell on the vulture's head. It burned his feathers. He was angered. He too began to fight.

At last they ceased. The lion said: "Different creatures of the bush cannot live together. It is against their nature. Therefore, we must live apart. We cannot share a meal at the same time. Henceforth, each must take his turn."

They separated, each one going his own way. They

remained apart. And now when the lion makes a kill he eats alone. Only when he is finished and goes away does the hyena come to eat. When the hyena goes away the vulture takes his turn.

Though all three were angered, it was the vulture who was most aggrieved, for the fire burned away the feathers from his head, and ever since that time he has been bald.

Ijapa and the Oba
Repair a Roof

IT came to the attention of a certain Oba, or chief, that while other people came, as they were supposed to, to mend his fences and cultivate his gardens, only Ijapa the tortoise did not fulfill his obligations. The Oba made it a principle that everyone should perform some kind of duty. There were some who served as soldiers. There were others who came several days each year to cultivate the ground or make bricks or build houses on the Oba's lands. But Ijapa did not appear. So the Oba sent for him. Ijapa came. He lay down on the ground as a mark of respect for the chief. The Oba was stern. He said: "Ijapa, I am displeased. You do not respect me. Others have come to do their work. Only you have failed to appear."

Ijapa said: "Great Oba, it is not disrespect. The only reason I did not come is that I felt I would be worthless."

The Oba was not taken in by Ijapa's words, for Ijapa had a reputation for clever talk. The Oba said: "Now that you are here, do not remain as motionless as a tree. Go and cut thatch leaves to mend the roof of my house."

58

As Ijapa went off to fetch leaves, people said: "Look, there is Ijapa. At last he has to work for the Oba like other people."

Ijapa said: "It is not I who works for the Oba, it is the Oba who works for me."

There was laughter. People said: "Ijapa's mouth cannot control itself."

Ijapa gathered the leaves and went to the house where the roof had to be repaired. Other people loitered nearby to watch him take orders from the Oba. The Oba himself was particularly offended by Ijapa's manner. He decided to see to it that Ijapa did his work properly, so he stood before the house and watched. He noticed that Ijapa was moving very slowly. He said: "Ijapa, begin the mending!"

Ijapa said: "Great Oba, I am beginning." He quickly climbed to the roof. "See," he said, "I am commencing the work." Now, Ijapa should have removed his waistcloth before going up, and he should have placed the newly cut thatch leaves on the roof before going up. When he arrived on the roof, he removed his waistcloth and said to the chief: "Great Oba, now I am beginning. Since you are there, have the kindness to take my waistcloth and hang it on the tree over there."

The Oba took Ijapa's waistcloth and hung it on a tree limb.

"You see, I am making progress," Ijapa said. "Now, if you will pass the thatch leaves up to me, the work will be half done."

The Oba was impressed with Ijapa's methodical and serious approach to repairing the roof. He picked up a bundle of thatch and passed it to Ijapa. "We progress, we progress!" Ijapa said. "Now another bundle!" The Oba was pleased at so much progress. He picked up another bundle and gave it to Ijapa. Then he picked up the third bundle. "One moment, Great Oba," Ijapa said. "Hold it for a moment." The Oba held the bundle. At last Ijapa said he was ready, and the Oba raised the bundle over his head and Ijapa took it.

All the people who loitered near the house saw the Oba take care of Ijapa's waistcloth and hand up the bundles of thatch one by one. They said: "Indeed, it is not Ijapa who works for the Oba, but the Oba who works for Ijapa!"

Because they liked what they saw, the people made a proverb:

"The day an Oba puts a person to work, that is the day he also should be put to work."

Sofo's Escape
from the Leopard

IN the north country, among the Hausa people, there was a boy named Sofo. His father was a Muslim teacher and his mother a weaver of fine cloth. As Sofo was their only child, nothing was too good for him. They dressed him in fine clothes and paid him great attention. But Sofo was bored with the village. What he liked most was to go out and explore the bush country. Often when someone looked for Sofo he was not to be found in the village at all. Instead, he would be out with his sling hunting birds or setting traps for small game or fishing in the river.

It worried his parents that Sofo was alone so much in the bush, for there were dangers there. They spoke of the leopards and snakes that he might encounter, but Sofo was not impressed. At last, because Sofo could not be deterred, his father prepared a charm for him to wear for protection. He wrote a saying from the Koran on a small piece of sheepskin. He wrapped it in leather and bound

61

the charm around Sofo's waist. After that they did not fear so much for his safety.

One morning Sofo took his sling and went out to hunt birds. Because of the charm he wore he felt secure, and he went to a distant place that he had never before explored. But he found no birds, and he went on. He walked until tiredness overcame him. Then he sat on a rock to rest.

Just at this moment a deer that had been sleeping nearby sprang to its feet, bellowed, and ran away. Sofo was startled. He, too, sprang to his feet and ran, leaving his sling behind. Although he had been exhausted only a moment before, fear gave him strength, and he ran at great speed, thinking only of the dangerous creature he had seen. He arrived at the village. People gathered around him. His mother came. They asked Sofo what had happened.

He said: "I was out there in the wild bush. A great leopard came from behind the rocks. It bellowed at me. I ran for my life. The leopard could not catch me. Now I have arrived safely at the village."

The people spoke in wonder about Sofo's escape from the leopard. His mother picked him up and carried him home. His father asked: "What is the cause of the excitement?"

His mother said: "Let us praise God! Our child was out among the rocks. A leopard came to seize him. He fled. The leopard could not catch him."

Sofo's father also said: "Praise to God!" He was happy. His son had been in grave danger, but now he was safe. He saw that Sofo was not carrying his sling. "Where is your sling for killing birds?" he asked.

Sofo was indignant. He had been pursued by a leopard, and his father was asking about his sling. He answered with a proverb: "A bearded man died in the fire, and you are asking what happened to his beard."

His father said: "You are right. Your safety is all that matters." Because his son had survived great danger, his father decided to give a thanksgiving feast for the village. Food was prepared. A beautiful new white cloth was placed around Sofo's shoulders. A large crowd came. Sofo's father praised God for the boy's safe homecoming. People gathered around Sofo asking for details about his adventure.

One person asked: "Sofo, is this the first leopard you have ever seen?" Another asked: "How large was it?" A third asked: "How long were its teeth?" They asked many questions, and Sofo began to describe his leopard.

"It was the first leopard I ever saw. It was as near as from here to there. He was ferocious. His color was brown. His sides were marked with white stripes. He was as fat as a full-grown sheep. On his head were long, terrible horns. And when he roared, he made a sound like this." Sofo imitated the bellowing of the deer.

The crowd around Sofo fell silent. They looked at the ground. They tried not to smile. One of them spoke to Sofo's father, saying, "What leopard ever made a sound like that? What leopard ever had horns on his head. What your son fled from was a deer."

Sofo's father took the new white cloth from Sofo's shoulders. The people went home.

Afterwards there came to be a proverb. Whenever a person talked too much and revealed the foolishness of his remarks, the proverb was quoted:

"Too much description spoiled Sofo's leopard."

How Ologbon-Ori
Sought Wisdom

IN a certain village there was a man named Ologbon-Ori. He himself had never been far from his village, but he had heard many travelers speak of the wonders and wisdom to be found in the outside world. Ologbon-Ori yearned to see what the world beyond the bush country was like and to obtain some of the wisdom that was to be found there. And one day after the yams had been harvested he decided to go on a journey with his small son to find some of it.

Ologbon-Ori had things prepared. He and his son bathed and put on their finest clothes. He fed his camel and watered him. Then he mounted the camel and seated his boy behind him. His friends stood at the trail as he departed, wishing him a safe journey. Ologbon-Ori and his son rode away.

In time they came to a town. There were many buildings. Many women were going and coming with produce on their heads. In the distance there was the hum of the marketplace. Ologbon-Ori rode to where the trading was going on. He was amazed at so much activity. "See," he said to his son, "around us is wisdom in great quantities. Let us see, let us learn."

Ologbon-Ori watched all the goings on with fascination. But soon he noticed that people were pointing at him and making comments. He listened. "What kind of man is this?" he heard someone say. "He makes his half-starved camel carry two persons." Someone else said: "Yes, he must come from the bush country. He has no feelings. See how exhausted his camel is."

When he had passed through the town, Ologbon-Ori said to his son: "You see, there are things to be learned in the world. I had not known it before, but a camel should not carry two people. So dismount, my son, and walk alongside."

The boy dismounted. He walked while his father rode. And in time they came to another town. As they passed through it, Ologbon-Ori marveled at the sights. But again he saw people pointing at him and making comments. He heard one man say: "See how the father rides while he makes the small child walk. Can such a man have a heart?" Another said: "Yes, it is so. Why should a strong man treat a boy this way?" A third man said: "He rides as though he were an Oba and the little one his slave."

Ologbon-Ori was troubled. He stopped, saying, "The knowledge of the world is hard to learn. How could we have gotten wisdom like this in our village?"

He dismounted and put his boy on the camel. The boy rode, and the father walked, and in this manner they came to the next town. It, also, was full of wonders. But once again Ologbon-Ori noticed that people were talking about him. "What is everything coming to," one man said, "when the young ride and the old must walk?" "Yes," another said, "is there no respect any more for the aged? Since when does the child go in comfort while the father's feet are covered with dust?"

This time Ologbon-Ori was greatly perplexed. He thought about it deeply. At last he said: "There is much to learn in the outside world, things we never dreamed of in the village. How lucky we are to have made this journey. It is clear that neither of us may ride the camel, else shame comes on one or the other. Let us walk, therefore, the father and son side by side."

So walking together and leading the camel by his halter, they arrived in the fourth town, intrigued by the wonders around them. But as it was before, so it was again. People

pointed, laughed, and made remarks. One said: "Look. A man, a boy, and a camel, walking together like friends." Another said: "Whenever before has anyone seen such idiots? They are footsore and tired, yet they walk. Why don't they mount that camel and ride like any sensible people would do?"

This time when Ologbon-Ori stopped to consider the matter, he remained in thought a long while. At last he said: "I believe our journey has come to an end. We have learned a great thing—that the wisdom of one town is the stupidity of another. Whatever a man does to please some-one will surely annoy others. Let us mount. Let us ride. Let us return whence we came." They mounted and rode back to their village in the bush country.

When they arrived, Ologbon-Ori's friends stood at the trail to greet him. They asked: "Where is it? Where is the wisdom of the world?"

Ologbon-Ori replied: "There is much wisdom to be found. I have returned with only a small portion of it. It is this:

" 'Seek wisdom, but do not throw away common sense.' "

Ijapa and Yanrinbo
Swear an Oath

As it is known to all, Ijapa was shiftless and did not tend his own garden. His wife Yanrinbo spent all her time making conversation with other women, sometimes in the market, sometimes on the trail, sometimes at the stream where the laundering was done. Between the two of them, nothing was ever put away for a time of need. There came a drought in the country, and food was scarce. Other people did not have enough food supplies to spare anything for Ijapa and his wife. They were faced with hunger.

Ijapa said: "Our neighbor Bamidele has a storage house full of yams. It is not right that he has yams while we have none."

He made a plan. And early one morning, before daylight, he awakened Yanrinbo. She took a large basket, and the two of them set out for Bamidele's place. When they approached the storage house, Ijapa ordered Yanrinbo to sit on his shoulders. She did this and placed the basket on her head. Then he went to the storage house. There

they filled the basket with yams, and with his wife sitting on his shoulders and the basket on her head, he returned the way he had come. When they arrived home, they emptied the basket and returned for more. The second time, like the first, Yanrinbo sat on Ijapa's shoulders with the basket on her head. They made many trips this way, until they had enough.

A few days later the neighbor, Bamidele, discovered that a large portion of his yams was missing. He saw footprints leading toward Ijapa's house. He inquired here and there. And at last he brought Ijapa and Yanrinbo before the chief and accused them of taking his yams.

Now, it was the custom to take persons accused of a crime to a particular shrine, where they would either admit their guilt or swear their innocence. If they confessed their misdeeds, they were punished according to the law. If they swore their innocence, they then drank a bowl of agbo, an herb drink prepared by the shrine priest. If the oath they had sworn was true, it was said, nothing would happen to them. But if they had sworn to a falsehood, the agbo would cause them to fall sick. In this way their guilt or innocence would become known.

The chief ordered Ijapa and Yanrinbo to appear before this shrine. The whole village came to watch the trial. Ijapa and Yanrinbo kneeled before the shrine while the priest made the agbo. When all was ready, Ijapa was called upon to swear his oath. He swore: "If I, Ijapa, the husband of Yanrinbo, ever stretched up my hand to remove yams from Bamidele's storage house, may I fall sick instantly and die."

Then Yanrinbo swore: "If I, Yanrinbo, wife of Ijapa, ever used my legs to carry me to Bamidele's storage house to steal yams, may I fall sick instantly and die."

The priest then gave Ijapa and Yanrinbo a large bowl of agbo to drink. They drank. They did not fall ill. Nothing at all happened. Seeing this, the chief said: "Their oaths were true. Therefore, release them." So Ijapa and Yanrinbo were released.

What they had sworn was not false, for Yanrinbo had not used her legs to get to the storage house. She had ridden on Ijapa's shoulders. And Ijapa had not raised his hands to carry away the yams. It was Yanrinbo who had raised her hands to balance the basket on her head.

Antelope's Mother:
The Woman in the Moon

NCE, in ancient times, there was a famine. The animals of the bush were hungry. They came together to see what could be done. Kiniun the lion was chief. He sat on his stool and listened while some said this and some said that. No one offered an easy solution. At last, Asa the hawk proposed that every creature in turn should offer up his mother to feed the community. It was agreed. Kiniun the lion said: "So it is. It has been arranged." He appointed Etu the antelope to be in charge of gathering food. As the antelope was thus honored, it fell to him to bring the first meat.

But Etu had no thought of killing his mother for food. Instead, he took her into the bush and then mounted to the moon, where he hid her. It was a place of plenty. The soil underfoot was custard powder, and the liquid that came from the springs was honey. The house posts were made of dried meat. Food was everywhere. It was arranged that when the antelope wished to visit his mother she would put down a rope for him to climb. He returned to earth. There he gathered rotted wood in the forest, cut it into small pieces, and seasoned it with oil, salt, and pepper. He cooked it and brought it to the other creatures, saying: "I have done what was required. Here is food."

The animals ate. They enjoyed the food. They said: "Antelope meat is good indeed." Time went on. The other animals did what was required of them. The buffalo, the hawk, the elephant, even the chief, Kiniun the lion, each in turn brought meat. Still there was not enough to eat. The animals grew thin. But Etu the antelope, when he was hungry, went to his mother on the moon. There he ate well.

Ijapa the tortoise noticed that Etu was fat. He said to the antelope: "You, my friend, of all the creatures of the bush, only you grow fat. How is it that you, too, are not hungry?" The antelope would not speak, for the tortoise was not trustworthy. But the tortoise persisted in his questions.

At last Etu said: "Very well. I will show you. Meet me in the bush tomorrow." Before the sun rose, the tortoise was waiting, calling on the antelope to hurry. Though it was still dark, the antelope came, and he led the tortoise to a certain place. There he sang:

"Woman in the moon, *alujan-kijan!*
Everyone has eaten his mother, *alujan-kijan!*
Even Kiniun the lion has done so, *alujan-kijan!*
Only I, Etu, have not done it, *alujan-kijan!*
Let down the rope, *alujan-kijan!*
So that your son may come up and eat, *alujan-kijan!*"

73

Antelope's mother let down the rope. The antelope and the tortoise grasped it, and the antelope's mother drew them to the moon. The tortoise began at once to eat the earth made of custard powder. Then he went to the spring and drank honey. When he could eat no more, he and the antelope returned to earth. There they parted, the tortoise going immediately to Kiniun the chief and reporting to him.

He said: "Etu has deceived us. His mother is on the moon, where food is plentiful. Have you not noticed how fat he is?"

The lion said: "The antelope is my agent. It is I who made him so. He would not deceive me."

The tortoise persisted. He said: "Oh, chief, if I have not told the truth, take my head!"

It was a solemn thing the tortoise said. So Kiniun replied: "Very well, we shall look into it."

The lion ordered the other animals to bring all their broken hoes and weapons. They did so. Then he sent for the antelope. He instructed the antelope to carry the broken hoes and weapons to a blacksmith in another town to have them repaired. The antelope put them on his back and started out. Because his load was heavy, he moved slowly, stopping often to rest. When Etu was gone, the chief said to the tortoise: "Now we shall look into the matter that you have spoken of. If you lied, I shall take your head. The words are yours. You have said it."

Ijapa led the animals into the bush. Making his voice sound like the antelope's, he sang:

74

"Woman in the moon, *alujan-kijan!*
Everyone has eaten his mother, *alujan-kijan!*
Even Kiniun the lion has done so, *alujan-kijan!*
Only I, Etu, have not done it, *alujan-kijan!*
Therefore, let the rope down, *alujan-kijan!*
So that your son may come up and eat, *alujan-kijan!*"

The antelope's mother lowered the rope. All the creatures gathered around and took hold of it. The antelope's mother raised them toward the moon. But there were many of them. Their weight was great, and antelope's mother was tired. So they dangled there, halfway between the moon and the earth.

The antelope returned from his journey. He found the countryside deserted. He went into the bush, and there he saw the other animals dangling in the sky. He called to his mother to cut the rope. She did so, and the creatures fell to earth. Many died, many were injured. As for the tortoise, his shell was broken into many pieces. He ordered the cockroaches to put his shell together. Because they were slow, he beat them. Because he struck them so hard, they became flat, and so they have remained. The tortoise's shell mended in time, but the cracks are still to be seen.

Because the rope had been cut, the antelope was not able to return to the moon. But on some nights you can see the figure of his mother shining in the darkness. She remains there, where the antelope took her for safety.

The Oba Asks
for a Mountain

I t was long ago. There was an Oba, or powerful chief, in the land of the Yoruba. He was not known for any virtues but for his love of war. It came to his ears that the kingdom of Ilesha was rich and prosperous. He decided he would loot Ilesha of its wealth, but he had no excuse to make war. So he sent messengers to Ilesha with a demand for tribute. The messengers arrived. They said: "The great Oba has sent us. He demands that a certain thing be done. If it is not done, his soldiers will come. They will make war. That is all. What is your answer?"

The people said: "What is this thing that is to be done? We will do it. We do not want war."

The messengers said: "The Oba has heard of the fine vegetables that are grown here. He wants a great quantity of these vegetables brought to him by the next festival day. But there is one thing. They must not be wrinkled and dried. They must be as fresh as when they are just taken from the earth."

77

The people said: "We shall bring them." But when the messengers had departed, the people said: "How can the vegetables be fresh when it takes a person fifteen days to go from here to there? They will be wrinkled and dried, and the Oba will make war upon us."

There was a man among them named Agiri-Asasa. He listened thoughtfully to what they said. "There is a way this thing can be done," Agiri-Asasa said. "Bring many pots and bowls. Dig up the vegetables with the earth around them and transplant them into these vessels. In this fashion they can be carried to the Oba."

As he described it, so it was done. They dug up the vegetables, earth and all, and carried them in pots and bowls to the distant town where the Oba lived. There they took the vegetables from the earth and brought them to the Oba's house. He was perplexed, for the vegetables

were fresh and sweet. He said nothing. He wondered what task he could give to the people of Ilesha that they could not perform, so that he would have an excuse for war.

The next morning as the people of Ilesha were preparing to leave, the Oba sent for them. He presented them with a thigh of beef, saying, "One thing more must be done if there is to be no war. This thigh of beef I entrust to you to keep for me. Return it to me on the third day before the yam harvest festival. But take care that it is returned to me as fresh as it is now. Do not allow it to become spoiled and moldy. Otherwise I shall send my soldiers to make war against Ilesha."

The people took the thigh of beef. They went out of the town. They talked. One said: "How can we do it? This meat will be spoiled before we reach home. It will soon be nothing but carrion." Another said: "Yes, it is so. The Oba means to destroy us."

Then Agiri-Asasa spoke, saying, "No, there is a way to deal with this matter. Let us take it with us a little way." So they took the thigh of beef and continued their journey. Even before the sun went down, they came to a place where a man was preparing to slaughter a bull. Agiri-Asasa said to him: "Do not hurry to slaughter the bull. Take this thigh of beef instead. We entrust it to your keeping. Three days before the yam festival we will come again. Slaughter your bull on that day and give us the thigh. Thus nothing will be lost, and it will save us from carrying this meat on the road." It was arranged.

On the third day before the festival, the people of Ilesha returned and received the thigh of the newly slaughtered bull. They carried it to the Oba, saying, "See, as you have directed, we return the beef thigh to you. It is as fresh as the day it was given to us." The Oba examined the meat. He was puzzled. He sent the people away.

He was angry. He determined to give Ilesha a task it could not perform. He sent messengers again to Ilesha. They stood in the marketplace and delivered the words of the Oba. "The great Oba has this to say. The people of Ilesha must bring him the mountain called Oke-Umo. Otherwise, he will be compelled to bring war to Ilesha." The people listened. They were worried. But they showed the messengers great respect. They fed them and gave them palm wine to drink.

When the messengers slept, the people discussed the matter. Agiri-Asasa had a plan. He said: "When morning comes, let us go to the mountain called Oke-Umo." When day arrived, ten thousand men of Ilesha escorted the messengers to the mountain. Every man had a carrying pad on his head. They surrounded the mountain in a circle. Agiri-Asasa called out: "Now lift the mountain and rest it on your carrying pads!" The ten thousand men tugged at trees and rocks, but they could not lift the mountain. At last Agiri-Asasa addressed the messengers this way: "Messengers of the great Oba, you see that we are willing to bring the mountain as the Oba has demanded. You see that we have ten thousand men ready to carry it. However, we cannot lift it. If the Oba will send his strongest men here to lift it onto our carrying pads, we will bring it to him without delay."

The messengers went home. They told the Oba. He listened. He said no more about the matter. He put Ilesha out of his mind.

Since that day, there has been a saying in Ilesha:

"There are people to carry the mountain,
But there is nobody to lift it."

The Journey to Lagos

wo travelers once met on the road to Lagos. They made friends with each other, saying, "The journey to Lagos is long. Let us travel together."

One man said: "Tell me your name so that I can call you by it."

The other man said: "I am called Do-Not-Advise-Me."

The first man said: "It is a good name. What does it mean?"

The second man said: "It tells its own meaning. And you, what are you called?"

The first man replied: "I am called Ride-No-One's-Back."

Do-Not-Advise-Me said: "I have never heard such a name before. But it has a good sound. What does it signify?"

Ride-No-One's-Back said: "It declares its own meaning. Let us not dwell on it."

The two friends, Do-Not-Advise-Me and Ride-No-One's-Back, walked together, and at night they slept side by side. The journey to Lagos took many days. The road was hard under their feet. Ride-No-One's-Back became lame. He limped. He began to walk slowly.

Do-Not-Advise-Me said: "Why are you limping?"

And Ride-No-One's-Back said: "My foot has been injured by the stones. Therefore I take short steps."

Do-Not-Advise-Me answered: "We are friends now, and we are going to the same place. Therefore I will carry you."

Ride-No-One's-Back declared: "No, you may not do it, for I am named Ride-No-One's-Back."

Do-Not-Advise-Me said: "If a man limps, another one carries him. It is always this way."

Ride-No-One's-Back said: "I must not ride. It is said in my name."

Do-Not-Advise-Me said: "Do not tell me the meaning of life. That is what my name says." They argued. Do-Not-Advise-Me said: "You, you limp; you walk slowly. You will never reach Lagos. I, I must reach Lagos quickly so that I can return to my village. Therefore I will carry you or we must travel alone."

Ride-No-One's-Back said: "I advise against it."

His friend replied: "Do not advise me."

So Ride-No-One's-Back climbed on the back of Do-Not-Advise-Me. They went forward. The road was hard. Do-Not-Advise-Me began to limp. He stopped, saying, "My foot is lame. Get down now so that I can rest."

But Ride-No-One's-Back could not get down. He said: "I cannot do it."

Do-Not-Advise-Me said: "Come down. I have never

83

heard that a man could not descend from another man's back."

Ride-No-One's-Back said: "I told you that in my village I was called Ride-No-One's-Back. You said, 'Do not tell me the meaning of life.' You insisted. I rode. But now I cannot come down."

Do-Not-Advise-Me said: "I am tired, I must rest. Therefore I will lie down." He lay down, his friend still affixed to his back. They could not sleep. When morning came, Do-Not-Advise-Me stood up. Ride-No-One's-Back was still there. Do-Not-Advise-Me said: "We have lain all night without sleeping. Come down now. Let us walk together."

Ride-No-One's-Back said: "I cannot come down."

Do-Not-Advise-Me said: "I cannot eat, I cannot drink, I cannot sleep, I cannot do anything. Only one thing I know, your weight on my back. It is killing me. Let us part ways. Each of us will go alone to Lagos."

Ride-No-One's-Back said: "You are my friend. Your trouble, I feel it. But I too have trouble. Before, I could get up or get down. I could eat or drink. Now that I am here, I cannot depart. My trouble is killing me also. I said to you, 'I must not ride.' But you, you persuaded me, saying that a name means nothing."

Do-Not-Advise-Me went on. He limped. He walked ever more slowly. The two friends no longer spoke, they were too weary. They entered the city of Lagos. Do-Not-Advise-Me fell down and died. Ride-No-One's-Back, he also died, still on his friend's back.

People gathered. They tried to separate the two. It was impossible. They took Do-Not-Advise-Me and Ride-No-One's-Back to the burial place. They placed them in a single grave.

There is a saying among the people:

"If trouble comes to a man, it comes also to his friend."

It is also said:

"If a good friend advises against a thing, do not do it."

Again it is said:

"If the meaning of a man's name is not to ride, he should not ride."

Ijapa Goes to
the Osanyin Shrine

GBE the guinea fowl had no farm of his own. He did not plant or cultivate. Instead, when he was hungry, he stole yams from the fields of a farmer named Odi. Agbe was careful. He took only one yam at a time, and the theft was not noticed. Ijapa the tortoise saw that the guinea fowl was well fed. He envied Agbe. He went to Agbe one day, saying, "Agbe, you have no land of your own. You do not work in the fields. How is it then that you never seem hungry?"

Agbe said: "I have a servant. His name is Odi. He plants for me."

Ijapa said: "You, a poor person like you has a servant?"

Agbe said: "It is so. Just as I said it, my servant plants for me."

Ijapa said: "I cannot swallow it. Your story has no legs to hold it up."

So Agbe took Ijapa to see for himself. They went to the edge of the field where the farmer was working.

"There he is," Agbe said. "He plants, he weeds, he takes care of my yams."

"Oh, but I am hungry!" Ijapa said. "Let us take some yams and cook them."

"Not now," Agbe said. "I have an understanding with my servant. It is agreed that the two of us shall not be in the field at the same time. When he is there, I remain in the bush. When I am there, he is home sleeping. This way we do not argue about things."

They waited. At last Odi the farmer left the field. Then Agbe and Ijapa went among the yams. Agbe dug up one yam. Ijapa dug up one yam.

Agbe said: "Now let us return to our homes."

But Ijapa protested. "You are so rich. Is one yam all you can offer to a guest on your farm?"

Agbe said: "I have an agreement with my servant. I take only one yam at a time."

"What foolishness!" Ijapa cried. "And how ungenerous you are!"

"Very well," Agbe said in disgust. "Take what you want." He left the field and returned to the bush with his single yam.

Ijapa dug up more yams. He made a bundle of them and placed it on his head. He dug still more. He made another bundle and put it on his back. Still he was not satisfied. He talked to himself, saying, "A wise man doesn't turn away from good fortune." He dug more yams and tied them to his neck with a piece of vine. He clutched yams with his hands and feet. He tried to leave the place, but his load was very heavy. He could scarcely move. Slowly, slowly. Every step made him pant. He became angry. He scolded the different parts of his body. He threatened them.

"Legs, if you don't move, no yams for you!
Neck, if you don't pull, no yams for you!
Back, if you don't carry, no yams for you!"

But nothing Ijapa said made any difference. The load was too great. He was bogged down in the middle of the field. He heard Agbe calling him, saying, "Leave the yams and go! My servant is coming!" But Ijapa would not consider leaving the yams behind. He stayed. He struggled.

When Odi the farmer returned, he found Ijapa lying helpless under the load of yams. He took the yams away. He tied Ijapa with a rope and dragged him across the fields to his house. He prepared to kill Ijapa with a stone. But Ijapa called out:

"Not this way is Ijapa killed!
Striking him with a stone is useless!
Bury him, instead, under a pile of grain,
Cover him with an earthen pot!"

The farmer listened. He considered the matter. Then he poured a basket of millet over Ijapa and covered him with a large pot.

The days came and departed. When a week had passed, Odi went to see if Ijapa was dead. He removed the pot. The millet was all gone. But Ijapa was alive and very fat. Odi was perplexed. He wondered what to do next to be rid of Ijapa. Ijapa called out:

"The grain was not fierce enough to kill Ijapa!
It failed to subdue him!
Ask a passing stranger to carry him away,
This will dispose of the matter!"

Many times Ijapa had been caught for his mischief. And always he talked his way to freedom. Though he was stupid in greed, he was clever in danger. The farmer listened to his words now. He thought about them. While he stood there, an Osanyin priest came along the trail on his way to his shrine. Odi thrust the tortoise into his hands, saying, "Sir, it is said that I should give you this." The Osanyin priest thanked him. He carried the tortoise to his shrine. There was a ritual being held at the shrine. It required a sacrifice. The Osanyin priest killed the tortoise because it was the only meat he had.

Before that time tortoises had never been sacrificed at the Osanyin shrine. But because of Ijapa's clever tongue it became a custom.

Ijapa and the
Hot-Water Test

Ⅰ T is said that one time Ijapa was called upon to come and help harvest the chief's fields. The idea interested Ijapa because he had neglected to care for his own fields, which therefore had produced nothing, while the chief's fields were full of yams. He thought about how he might use the occasion to fill his empty storehouse. A plan came to him. In the night he went to the chief's fields and dug a deep hole. He made the opening small at the top, and he sprinkled leaves and grass around the opening to disguise it. Then he carried away the dirt from the hole and threw it into the bush.

Morning came. Ijapa went to the chief's house, saying, "Here I am." Opolo the frog was already there, as were Ekun the leopard, Ekute the bush rat, Ewure the goat, Agbonrin the deer, and many others. They went out to the chief's fields to dig yams. Now, the other workers put the yams they dug into their baskets and carried them to the chief's storehouse. But Ijapa, he put a yam into his basket, then dropped a yam into the hole he had dug the night before. He put another yam into his basket and dropped another one into the hole. For each one he put in the basket he put another in the hole. Some of the workers scolded him for being slow, but Ijapa said: "I have great respect for the chief's yams. I handle them gently so as not to bruise them." The work went on. At last all the yams were harvested. The workers went home.

That night when darkness came, Ijapa took his wife and children to the place where he had hidden the yams. They went back and forth many times, each carrying as many yams as he could, until the hole was empty. Ijapa's storehouse was full. He was pleased.

But when daylight came, servants of the chief found Ijapa's hole. They found the path he and his family had made while going back and forth. They followed the path to Ijapa's storehouse. There they saw the yams, and they returned to report their discovery to the chief. The chief sent for Ijapa. He spoke sternly. "Ijapa, it is reported that you have taken yams from my field."

Ijapa said: "Oh, great chief, I came to help you with your harvest. I labored in the hot sun. I brought yams to your storehouse. Then I returned home. Now you reproach me. It is not I who has taken your yams."

The chief said: "Ijapa, your habits are widely known, and in addition there is a path from my fields to your storehouse."

Ijapa said: "Oh, sir, I went to your fields to work for you, I returned. Could this little walking have made a path? If there is such a path, it was made by others to discredit me. Were there not other persons in the fields also?"

The chief said: "There are no paths from my fields to their houses, only to yours. Therefore, suspicion falls on you. If you are innocent, we shall discover it. Let us prepare for the hot-water test. Tomorrow the people will assemble. We shall come to the truth of the matter."

The next day the people gathered in front of the chief's house, where a large pot of water was heating over a fire. When the water began to boil, the chief said: "Ijapa has been accused of stealing yams. He denies it. For this reason he will take the test. He will drink a bowl of the boiling water. If he is guilty, he will feel great pain. If he is innocent, he will not be harmed. In this way we shall know the truth. Let us begin."

Ijapa spoke, saying, "Oh, sir, though I will be proved innocent, you still will not know who has taken your yams. There were many persons there. Let them all be tested."

The chief considered it. He said: "This is good advice. Let everyone who was in the fields take the test."

Ijapa now became very helpful, as though he were the chief's assistant. He ordered that the pot be removed from the fire. "Place it here," he said, "so that the chief may see it from where he sits." They moved the pot of water from the fire as Ijapa directed.

"Because I am the youngest," Ijapa said, "it is I who should serve the water."

The chief agreed. So Ijapa took the bowl, filled it with hot water from the pot, and served it to Opolo the frog.

Opolo drank. The hot water burned him inside. He cried out in pain. Ijapa filled the bowl again. He presented it to Ekute the bush rat. Ekute drank. The water scalded his mouth. He cried out. Tears came to his eyes. Ijapa re-filled the bowl and handed it to Ewure the goat. Ewure drank. He cried. Ijapa gave hot water to Ekun the leopard. Ekun drank. He moaned in pain, and tears flowed from his eyes. Each person drank; each person suffered.

Then it came to be Ijapa's turn. The chief said: "All these persons have taken the test. All share the guilt. Now it is Ijapa's moment for guilt or innocence."

Ijapa said: "I, Ijapa, am innocent. Yet I am the one who was accused. Therefore, I shall drink the largest portion of the hot water. In this way I shall prove beyond doubt that I did not commit the crime. The bowl is too small. Therefore, bring me a large calabash."

The chief sent for a calabash. Ijapa filled it to the brim.

He carried it to the chief, saying: "See it, great chief, see how full the calabash is!"

The chief replied: "I see it. You do well, Ijapa."

Ijapa carried the calabash back and forth, saying, "Family of the chief, see how full the calabash is!"

The chief's family called out: "We see it. You do well, Ijapa!"

"Men of the village," Ijapa chanted, "see how full the calabash is!"

The men of the village called out: "We see it. You do well, Ijapa!"

"Women of the village," Ijapa sang, "see how full the calabash is!"

The women of the village answered: "We see it. You do well, Ijapa!"

"Boys of the village," Ijapa chanted, "see how full the calabash is!"

The boys chanted back: "We see it. You do well, Ijapa!"

"Girls of the village," Ijapa chanted, "see how full the calabash is!"

"We see it. You do well, Ijapa!" the girls replied.

Ijapa showed his calabash of water to this one and that one, each in turn, as evidence of the large amount of hot water he would drink. They could see that Ijapa was not shrinking from the ordeal. But Ijapa spent a great deal of time at this business, and the entire village was constantly singing, "We see it. You do well, Ijapa!"

Meanwhile, the water in the calabash was getting cool. At last the chief said: "Ijapa, we have declared ourselves enough. You do well. But now let us get on with it."

So Ijapa drank. Because the water had become cool, it did not pain him. He emptied the calabash. The chief nodded his approval. Ijapa said: "You have seen it. I did not cry out. Tears did not come from my eyes. How then can I be guilty?" And as an additional proof of his innocence, Ijapa jumped into the pot from which the water had come. The water in the pot also was cool. Ijapa made sounds of pleasure. Then he came out. He said to the chief: "As you see, it was not I who committed the crime. Surely it must be Opolo, and Ekute, and Ewure, and Ekun, and Agbonrin who are guilty, for it was they who felt the pain."

The other creatures protested, but the chief agreed with Ijapa. Thus it was that the chief found all of them except Ijapa guilty of the theft of his yams.

Since then, whenever a person tries to absolve himself of a bad action by putting the fault on others, people say:

"When Ijapa accuses the whole community,
He himself must have something to hide."

Ogungbemi and the
Battle in the Bush

IT is said that in the beginning there was neither day nor night. There was only a grayness over the earth.

In those times there lived a wealthy man by the name of Ojalugba. Among his slaves was a boy called Ogungbemi. Ojalugba, in an unreasonable mood one day, sent Ogungbemi into the bush to get a bundle of wood as high as his head. Ogungbemi went into the bush. He gathered wood. He stacked it till it was as high as his head. He tied it into a bundle. But it was too heavy. He could not lift it from the ground. He began to cry, for he knew Ojalugba would punish him.

At this moment a strange and terrifying person appeared. Ogungbemi was frightened. His crying stopped.

The terrifying person said: "My name is Fearsome."

Ogungbemi's tongue was dry from fright. He could not speak.

Fearsome said: "Your master has given you too great

a load to carry. If you say nothing about the matter, I will help you. But if you tell the village that Fearsome helped you with your task, I will come after you and take you into the bush."

Ogungbemi spoke at last. He said: "Help me, then. I shall say nothing."

Fearsome raised the bundle and set it on Ogungbemi's head. He made the load light. Ogungbemi carried it back to the house of Ojalugba as though it were nothing more than a small basket of cotton. He set it down. The people saw him. They wondered about it, for it was a load too great for a full-grown man. Some of them tried to lift it, but they couldn't raise it from the ground. They said: "The boy had help from a spirit of the bush."

Ogungbemi would not speak about the matter. He did not wish to be carried off by Fearsome. The news was

carried to Ojalugba. He came out of his house. He scolded Ogungbemi. He demanded to know how Ogungbemi had carried an impossible load. Still Ogungbemi was silent. Ojalugba became angry. He said: "I have many slaves. One more or one less, what do I care? I am rich. I want no slave who is silent when I command him to speak. Therefore, speak. If you do not speak, I will have you beaten and thrown into the river."

Ogungbemi was afraid. He spoke. He said: "I was in the bush. I couldn't lift the bundle of wood. I cried. The bush spirit came. His name is Fearsome. He made the bundle light. Thus, I carried it. But Fearsome told me not to speak of it, otherwise he would come and take me off into the bush."

Ojalugba said: "This bush spirit will never have you. I will see to it." He sent his servants and other people of the village to guard the fields and the houses. They took their weapons and stood guard.

But Fearsome came. He approached the village. He saw the men waiting to drive him off. He sprinkled a magic powder on the ground, and everyone in the village fell asleep. The guards also slept. Fearsome went to the house where Ogungbemi was hiding. He picked up Ogungbemi and departed. Ogungbemi awoke. He began to sing:

> "Saworo-jin-winni-jin-winni-saworo!
> Why is the village asleep?
> The cocks have stopped crowing,
> The house fires have stopped smoking,
> The women have stopped making fufu,

The men have stopped hoeing,
The marketplace is silent.
Ojalugba, rescue me!
Saworo-jin-winni-jin-winni-saworo!"

Ojalugba heard the song. He arose and awakened the
guards. They pursued Fearsome into the bush. They
caught him. There was a struggle. Fearsome took a packet
of magic powder from his waistcloth. He poured powder
on the ground. Instantly, darkness came over the world.

But the guards also carried a magic powder. They
threw some of it on the earth, and instantly it became
light.

Fearsome poured more of his powder on the earth, and
darkness came again. The guards poured magic powder
and the light returned. Fearsome poured powder and
blackness came.

When the magic powders were gone, they wrestled.
Their bodies became entangled. They struggled many
days. Gradually, as time passed, they became bush ropes,
the wild vines that twist and tangle themselves together
in the bush country. Ogungbemi, in the midst of the
fighting, turned into a swarm of ants that crawled up and
down the twisting bush ropes.

To this day the struggle has not ended. The bush ropes
are still there, and the ants crawl forever up and down.
The magic powders thrown upon the ground by Fearsome and the men of the village, they changed everything.
It became light, then dark, then light, then dark. Whereas
once there was only grayness in the world, now there are
day and night. First one, then the other. It never stops.

The Quarrel Between
Ile and Orun

Because the earth and the sky are now far apart does not mean that they were always so. Once the earth and sky were near to one another.

Before, before, in ancient times, Ile the earth and Orun the sky were close in friendship. They were hunters, and they often went together in search of game. There was no quarreling between them. They regarded each other as equals in all respects.

One day Ile and Orun went into the bush to search for meat. They followed the antelope trails, they followed the trails of the wild pigs, they looked for birds, but they found nothing. The day stretched out. They became hungry and tired. They became irritable. At last, when darkness was beginning to fall, they killed a bush rat. They roasted it. And when it was time to eat, they began to argue.

Ile said: "I shall take the first portion. I was here before there was a sky. I am the elder. Therefore the first portion belongs to me."

Orun said: "On the contrary, I was here before the earth was formed. It is I who am the elder. Therefore, the first portion belongs to me."

They argued this way, and the discussion became bitter. Orun the sky was offended. He said: "Why should we be friends? Friends do not treat each other this way. I am leaving you. The bush rat, keep it for yourself."

He arose. He departed from the place. Thus, the sky and earth became far apart. Before this happened, people had harvested their crops with ease. Food had been abundant. But now that the sky had moved away from the earth, the rain did not fall. Wells dried up. Crops did not grow. Where once there had been rivers, there now was only desert. Creatures of the bush thirsted and died.

At last a meeting was called to discuss the situation. The bush creatures decided that a messenger should be sent to Orun the sky, along with the bush rat that had caused the trouble. A certain bird was selected. He took the bush rat and tried to reach the sky with it, but he failed. The sky was too far away. Another bird tried. He also failed. Many birds tried, but they could not reach the place where Orun lived. At last Igun the vulture volunteered. The other creatures jeered, for the vulture was sluggish and clumsy. One said: "If our finest fliers have not been able to reach Orun, how then will the vulture ever do it?" Others said: "Yes, that is true." But the vulture was the only bird that had not tried. So they gave him the bush rat and sent him on his way. As he began his flight, the vulture sang:

"Earth and Sky,
    They went hunting,
    They killed a bush rat.
    Ile said he was the elder,
    Orun said he was the elder.
    Then Sky moved away.
    Yams stopped growing,
    The maize had no grains,
    Mothers searched for water,
    Babies cried."

Igun the vulture sang this way until he reached the sky.
Orun heard the song. He was sorry about what was happening. He received the bush rat from Igun. And in return he gave the vulture a packet of magic red powder
to take back with him. Orun explained carefully that a
tiny amount of the powder, when blown into the air,
would bring rain. The vulture took the present from

Orun and began his long descent to earth. But on the way down he opened the packet of magic powder. All the powder blew away. The light faded, and it became like night. The rain began to fall. There was a violent storm. On the earth the wind tore down trees and houses, the rivers overflowed, and villages were washed away by flood waters. There was destruction on every side.

When the storm was over, the creatures of the bush found the vulture and asked him what had happened. "It was the package of magic red powder," the vulture said. "I opened it a little. The wind blew it away." The bush creatures were angered. They attacked Igun. They struck him many times on the head.

In the old days, the vulture had feathers on his head, but because they beat him so hard the feathers fell out. Ever since then he has been bald. And ever since that time the vulture has lived apart. No one gives him shelter. As for food, he eats only what other creatures leave behind when they have eaten plenty.

Ijapa Demands Corn Fufu

HERE was a famine in the land. Food was hard to find, and the animals of the bush grew thin. Only Aja the dog was not overcome with hunger. Ijapa the tortoise saw that the dog was well fed. Indeed, Aja was fat, and Ijapa said to his family: "I will follow Aja and find his hoard of food. Then we also shall be fat."

One day Aja went into the bush. Ijapa followed. Aja went far. Ijapa walked behind. Aja came to a great tree in the bush. He sang a song. Something fell from the tree. Aja picked it up and departed. When Aja was gone, Ijapa approached the tree. He saw that it was laden with corn fufu. He called out: "Tree, give me some of what you have!" Nothing happened. He said: "Tree, give me a corn fufu or I will kick you!" Nothing happened. Ijapa kicked the tree. He cried out. His foot hurt him. He tried to climb, but he could not do it because his legs were too short. At last he went home. He told his family: "That Aja has powerful medicine. He made a corn fufu fall from a tree. That is why he isn't hungry. I will find out the secret."

In the morning he went to Aja's house. He said: "Aja, you are fat. I saw you at the corn fufu tree. Today I will go there with you."

Aja was worried. He said: "No, it cannot be."

Ijapa said: "Then I will announce it in the village. I will make the secret known everywhere."

Aja said: "Very well. If that is the way the matter goes, come then."

Ijapa picked up a basket. Aja said: "No, leave the basket."

Ijapa became angry. He said: "What kind of greedy person are you? You have a guest, but you do not permit him to bring a basket. So it shall be. As you see, then, I do not bring the basket. But let us hurry. My mouth aches for corn fufu."

They went into the bush. They approached the tree. Aja sang:

> "Corn fufu are plentiful,
> They hang in great numbers.
> May one drop on me,
> May two drop on me.
> Corn fufu are plentiful."

One corn fufu dropped from the tree. Ijapa grabbed it. Another fell. Aja took it. He said: "Now let us go."

But Ijapa would not go. He said: "How stupid to stop with only two! The tree is full of corn fufu. Let us take many."

Aja said: "No, we have been given one corn fufu each. That is all."

Ijapa said: "Just one more then."

Aja said: "No, we must take only a little. That way the corn fufu is plentiful."

Ijapa said: "But I am a family man. There are many stomachs to fill at home."

Aja refused to ask for more, but he gave his own corn fufu to Ijapa. Ijapa took his two corn fufu to a place in the bush. He ate them. He went home. The children said: "Father, where are the corn fufu?"

Ijapa said: "Do not be greedy! Who has corn fufu to give out these days? Tomorrow I will bring some."

The next morning Ijapa took a large basket. He went by himself to the tree in the bush. He stood beneath the tree and sang Aja's song, just as he had heard it. But he did not ask for one corn fufu or two corn fufu. He asked for *all* the corn fufu. The tree made a groaning sound. It tilted. The roots snapped in the ground, making sounds like musket fire. The tree fell on Ijapa, burying him under a huge pile of corn fufu. Thus Ijapa met his end. In greed he lived, and greed buried him.

The Wrestlers

N Emir who ruled in the north country decided one time to invite a creature of the bush to live in his palace. He sent a messenger to tell the animals what he had in mind. The messenger instructed the animals to appoint someone to go back with him to live with the Emir.

They discussed the matter. The elephant volunteered to live with the Emir. The lion volunteered. The boar volunteered. The goat volunteered. Each creature, in turn, asked to be appointed. They could not agree. They began to argue. Their tempers became hot. At last someone made a suggestion.

"It appears," he said, "that the matter cannot be decided this way. Therefore let us have a wrestling contest. The person who is undefeated will be chosen."

So a wrestling contest began. The elephant wrestled with the boar and threw him down. The lion wrestled with the elephant and threw him down. The goat wrestled with the lion and threw him down. At last, only the hyena was undefeated and only the cat remained to challenge him.

"Let us wrestle no more," the hyena said. "The cat is too weak to wrestle me. I will go to live with the Emir."

But the cat said: "No, it is not yet decided. Let us wrestle together."

They approached each other. They grappled. The hyena was strong. He seized the cat and threw him into the air. But the cat did not fall on his back. He landed on his feet. They grappled again. Once more the hyena threw the cat into the air. Once more the cat landed on his feet. It angered the hyena. He said: "I have thrown the cat. I have won."

But the other animals answered: "Not yet. You must throw your opponent on his back."

So again the hyena grappled with the cat. Again he threw, and again the cat landed on his feet. The contest

went on and on. The hyena could not do what was necessary. At last, greatly tired, he fell down. The cat was proclaimed the winner. The hyena was strong, but he did not have the talent to win.

The cat went with the messenger to the palace of the Emir. The Emir welcomed him. He gave the cat a place in the palace. The cat is still there. He is treated like a guest. He rubs against the feet of the Emir without reproach, even while the Emir is engaged in great affairs of state. This is how the cat came out of the bush to live with man.

Because of what was learned about him in the wrestling match, people made a proverb:

"The back of the cat never touches the ground."

How the People of Ife
Became Scattered

HE old ones say that Ife, in the land of the Yorubas, was the first town in which mankind lived. In those days all people were dark-skinned. They all spoke a single language—Yoruba. And there was no poverty. If men needed something, they had only to inform God's messenger, and he would bring the matter to God's attention. God provided whatever was asked of him. There were enough yams, fruit, corn, and millet for all. No person had more or less in life than any other person in Ife.

But one day when the people were together in the market, a man asked a question. He said: "Everyone in Ife is the same. Why should it be this way? Look about you. Everyone has the same color of skin. All men look alike. No man owns more or less than the next one. Is this tolerable?"

People began to think about it. They said: "It is true. Why does everyone have the same of everything? Shouldn't each person have something different?"

And so first one man, then another, sought out God's

messenger and asked for something that other people didn't have. One wanted a larger house. A second wanted more yams. A third wanted money. Another wanted servants and slaves. Some asked for lighter skins. They complained about the sameness of everything.

Day by day the messenger went back and forth carrying the complaints and requests. At first God listened patiently to what the messenger told him. But after a while he became irritated. He sent his messenger to Ife to put an end to the complaints. The messenger told the people: "I have taken your complaints to God. He has considered everything. He doesn't like the way things are going. In the beginning he arranged it so that you would all be equal in appearance and in the things you own. He did this so that there would be no dissension. The things you want now will bring conflict to the human race."

The people of Ife did not listen. They demanded things. They argued. The messenger debated with them. But the men and women of Ife declared that unless they received the things they wanted they would revolt and have nothing more to do with God. So the messenger left Ife and went to report to God on the way things were going. God listened. He said: "Very well. Let them have what they want."

The messenger came again to Ife. The man who wanted a brown skin, he received it. One who wanted a white skin, it was given to him. Some people received land, some received servants and slaves, some received money. The messenger gave everything out and went away. The people began to quarrel among themselves about who had received the most. Some complained that they deserved more. People of one color looked with suspicion on those who were lighter or darker than themselves. Whereas once they had spoken only Yoruba, now they began to speak in different languages. Some spoke Swahili, some Ibo, some Hausa, some Arabic. It became difficult for them to understand one another. So they scattered. Some went to the north, some to the east, some to the west, some to the south. They settled in different places and became the tribes of the world.

Once, in the town of Ife, all men had the same of everything. After they dispersed, nothing was equal, and to this day they remain afflicted with envy, suspicion, and the desire to have more than others have.

How Moremi Saved
the Town of Ife

N ancient times it was not known in Ife that human beings lived in other places. Around Ife were farmlands, and beyond the farmlands in all directions was thick forest. No person in Ife had ever gone through the forest to see what was on the other side. It was taken for granted that beyond the forest there was only more forest and that Ife was the only place with human life.

Nevertheless, there was another town called Ile-Igbo. The people of Ile-Igbo also believed that they were the center of all things. Surrounding their town were farmlands, and beyond the fields was the forest. Just as the people of Ife had never heard of Ile-Igbo, so the people of Ile-Igbo had never heard of Ife.

But there was a hunter in Ile-Igbo who became lost in the forest. He wandered many days without knowing where he was, and by accident he came to Ife. He did not dare to go into the town because he was afraid. He went back into the forest, and when at last he found his way again to Ile-Igbo, he told the Oba what he had seen. It

113

seemed like an impossible story, for the Oba had never heard that there was another town in the world. The Oba, therefore, sent two messengers to verify the hunter's report. They went into the forest and beyond. They found Ife. They saw that the story was true. They observed the people. They took note of the prosperous farms. And afterwards they returned to Ile-Igbo and told the Oba about the wonders of Ife. "The people there are rich and happy," the messengers said. "Their gardens are bursting with food. Their granaries and storehouses are full of yams and grain. Their marketplace is a place of wonders, and people are busy buying and selling things we have never even seen in Ile-Igbo."

The Oba pondered on what he had heard. Ife had everything while Ile-Igbo had little. The gardens of Ile-Igbo were poor, and the people were not well off. In Ile-Igbo there was much poverty, and people worried constantly about having food enough to last from one harvest to the next.

The Oba called his ministers and advisers to meet in council. They talked about Ife and its wealth. They spoke of Ile-Igbo's poverty. And it was decided at last that an expedition must be sent to Ife to obtain food and bring it to Ile-Igbo. A plan was devised. Men were chosen to carry out the raid. They were dressed in weird costumes made of raffia and grass so that they resembled wild monsters of the forest. They were called egunguns.

The army of egunguns went through the forest and entered the town of Ife. The people of Ife were frightened. Never had they seen such creatures. They ran away in

fright. The egunguns went to the storehouses and took away all the food they could carry. They returned home. The people of Ile-Igbo were delighted. Now there was plenty of food, and they no longer worried about the future.

But after the food was eaten, there was hardship again. It was decided to send another expedition to Ife. The egunguns went out again. They came into Ife with wild cries, and the people of the town scattered and ran into the bush to save themselves. The egunguns brought more food home to Ile-Igbo. It went on this way year after year. The people of Ife worked in their fields and harvested their crops, and then the egunguns came out of the forest and emptied the storehouses and granaries. Life in Ife became hard. Some people became hungry. Some people starved.

There was a woman in Ife called Moremi. She proposed that when the forest spirits came again she would remain behind in the town to learn more about them. Her family and her friends protested. They said the forest creatures would take her away. But Moremi insisted.

The food was gathered and put in the storehouses. It was almost time for the egunguns to come again. Moremi went to the sacred brook called Esinminrin. There she pleaded for help against the egunguns. She pledged that if the sacred brook would bring her safely out of the hands of the forest monsters, she would offer her small son, Oluorogbo, as a sacrifice.

The days went by. Then the egunguns came again. They swarmed into Ife with wild cries, and the people of the town fled. Only Moremi stayed behind. The egunguns took the food. Seeing Moremi, they took her also. And when they arrived at Ile-Igbo, they brought Moremi to their Oba. He was pleased with her appearance. He liked her. He took her and made her one of his wives. Moremi waited for an opportunity to escape. Months passed. People began to forget that she came from Ife. They no longer thought about it.

One night when Moremi was with the Oba, she brought him much palm wine. He drank heavily. It made his senses dull, and a deep sleep came on him. Moremi clothed herself in rags so that she looked like a beggar, and in the darkness of the night she escaped into the forest and found her way back to Ife. There was happiness in the town when she returned. People gathered. There was singing and dancing. Moremi told the people what she had seen in Ile-Igbo. Their surprise was great when they learned that the egunguns were not forest monsters at all but only men dressed in raffia and grass. They discussed the matter, and they decided how they would deal with the egunguns.

Time passed. One day the egunguns appeared again. They came with wild cries into the town. The people were waiting for them. They came out of the houses with lighted torches and set fire to the grass costumes of the egunguns. The egunguns were aflame. They ran this way and that, some dying, some escaping back into the forest. They never came to Ife again. There was a festival, and the people honored Moremi for her act of courage that made victory possible for Ife.

But Moremi had one more act of courage to perform. She had pledged to give her son Oluorogbo to the sacred brook. She took her son from her house. She carried him to the brook, the people of the town walking behind. There was a ritual there at the edge of the water. They gave the boy. They left him lying there at the place of sacrifice and returned to the town. Moremi was filled with grief.

When they were gone, a golden chain descended from the sky. Oluorogbo sat up. He took hold of the chain, and he was raised into the sky, where he lives to this day. So it was told. Moremi's courage saved the town of Ife. She paid her debt to the sacred brook Esinminrin, and Oluorogbo went to live with the god of the sky.

The Staff of Oranmiyan

WHEN the ancient town of Ife was young, there was a warrior king by the name of Oranmiyan. When the enemies came to make war, it was Oranmiyan who led Ife's warriors into the battle. Where the fighting was hardest, that was where Oranmiyan was to be seen. It was he who taunted the enemy loudest, and it was he who struck down their greatest fighters. He was first on the battlefield and the last to leave it. The heroes in ancient Ife were many, but Oranmiyan stood above them all, and his name was known in faraway places. Many times the chiefs of other lands tried to defeat Ife and make it pay tribute, but Ife could not be subdued.

Time moved on, and Oranmiyan became older. Other heroes, when they had lived, then they died. Oranmiyan did not die. Instead, when his time came, he went to the marketplace in the center of the town. He said to the people of Ife: "I leave you now, but I do not die. When trouble falls upon Ife, I will return. When heroes are needed, call me." He stuck his staff into the earth. It turned into stone. He stamped on the ground with his foot. The ground opened. He went down. The ground closed behind him. Thus, when his time came, Oranmiyan left Ife. But his stone staff stood there in the market as a reminder of his pledge.

In a distant place it was heard that the great hero-king Oranmiyan was no longer in Ife, so an army was sent to conquer the town. When the people of Ife saw the enemy approaching, the warriors armed themselves and prepared to fight. They went to the place where Oranmiyan had placed his staff, and they called for him to join them in the battle. The ground opened. Oranmiyan came out, holding his weapons. He led the warriors of Ife to the place of combat. They fought. The enemy were defeated. They turned and fled. The men of Ife returned singing to their town. Oranmiyan went to the marketplace. The ground opened. He entered, descending into the earth. The ground closed behind him.

Many times it happened that Ife was threatened by an enemy, but because of Oranmiyan, Ife was never defeated.

Then one time there was a festival in the town. People danced and sang, and the men drank much palm wine. They became drunk. Someone said: "Oranmiyan should be here to dance and sing with us." Others said: "Yes, it is so." They went to the place of Oranmiyan's staff. They called on Oranmiyan to join them. At first they said: "Oranmiyan, come and dance with us." But he did not appear. Then they said: "Oranmiyan, come swiftly, the town is in danger." The ground opened. Oranmiyan came out, his weapons in his hands. Because it was night,

119

he believed that the men in the marketplace were the enemy. He began fighting. He killed many men of Ife. He pursued those who ran. The killing went on. The dawn came. Oranmiyan saw that he had been fighting with the men of the town. He saw the bodies on the ground. Grief came to him. He said: "I was told Ife was in danger. Therefore, I came. I killed my comrades. From now on I shall not fight. I shall not come again to Ife." He entered the earth. It closed behind him. What he said was true. He was never again seen in Ife.

The staff that Oranmiyan placed in the ground, now turned to stone, still stands in the marketplace. Every year the people of Ife gather there and hold a service for him, recalling his greatness and how drunkenness in the town caused him to disappear forever.

The First Woman
to Say "Dim"

IT was not always that wives acknowledged that their husbands were in fact husbands. In ancient times, it is said, women addressed their husbands as *nwokem*, meaning "friend." As for the men, they addressed their wives properly, called them *nwayem*—"my wife"— and they were not happy to hear their wives calling them merely "friend," for a woman may have many friends but only one husband. Today women acknowledge this, but it was not always so.

It is said that it was a man named Maka who was responsible for making women say *dim*, "my husband." He had many times tried to get his wife to say *dim*, but she would not do it. All she would say was *nwokem*, "my friend." He went to a *babalawo*, a priest who could perform acts of magic, and pleaded that he be given the power to make his wife say *dim*. The *babalawo* said: "Who has the magic to make a woman do what she does not want to do?"

But Maka pressed him, saying, "Is it right that a woman

121

should call her husband 'friend'? You, does your wife acknowledge you as 'husband'?" The *babalawo* considered the matter. He made a powerful magic bundle, which he gave to Maka. Maka went home.

The next morning he arose early and told his wife they were going into the bush to look for herbs and roots. They set out. When they reached a distant place in the bush, Maka said: "Wait here. I am going just a little beyond. I will return soon."

He went just a little beyond, and there, with the magic he had acquired from the *babalawo*, he turned himself into a large snake. Then he returned to where his wife was waiting. He crawled around her, threatening to bite, but she was unimpressed. She picked up a stick and struck at him. He crawled away.

Then Maka turned himself into a river. The river rushed angrily to the place where the woman waited, swirling around her and threatening to carry her away. But Maka's wife merely moved to higher ground, where the river couldn't follow, and she didn't bother to call Maka for help.

The river slipped back into the brush, and Maka turned himself into a roaring brush fire. The fire swept down on Maka's wife, surrounding her, consuming the tall grass and crackling in the tops of the trees. Closer and closer the fire came to the woman. She tried to go this way and that way, but the fire was all around her. She felt the scorching heat. There was no way to escape. At last she cried out: "*Nwokem!* My friend!" But Maka was nowhere to be seen. The fire came closer. Smoke was in

her mouth. She called out more loudly: *"Nwokem! Nwokem!* My friend!" Still there was no Maka. Now the flames were reaching toward her clothing. At last, in desperation, she cried: *"Dim! Dim!* My husband! My husband!"

The fire died away. Maka appeared. They looked for herbs. They found them. They returned home.

Thereafter, Maka's wife never again called him "friend." She called him *dim,* "my husband." It became the custom everywhere. So it remains.

Why No One
Lends His Beauty

EFORE, before, in the beginning of things, people wore their beauty as they wore clothes. It is said that there was a girl named Shoye who possessed beauty that was the pride of her village. Wherever she went, people said: "When before has anyone seen such beauty?"

There was another girl in the village named Tinuke. She did not have such beauty to wear. She envied Shoye. She went to her one day and said: "I must go on a journey for my family. I have no beauty. Lend me your good looks until I return." Shoye did not hesitate. She gave her good looks to Tinuke. Tinuke took the beauty. Her face shone with it. She walked gracefully. She left the village and went on her journey.

People who saw her said: "Whenever has such a beautiful girl been seen?" She went to the town where a chief lived. His friends told him: "There is a girl in the town. She comes from another place. She has great beauty." The chief sent for Tinuke. He saw her beauty. He took her as a wife. She did not return to her own village.

Shoye waited. She was very ugly. When she went to the market, people said: "When before has anyone seen such ugliness?"

Tinuke did not return. Shoye's friends said: "Tinuke has surely stolen your beauty. You must find her." So Shoye went in search of Tinuke. She came to the town of the chief.

People said: "What ugliness! She has a hideous face! It will bring bad luck on us. Send her away!" But Shoye would not go away. She heard that Tinuke now lived in the house of the chief. She went there. She asked for Tinuke. Tinuke would not come. She hid behind the walls of the chief's compound.

When the chief passed through his gate, he saw Shoye there. He said: "Who is the girl with the ugly face crouching before my estate?"

His guards said: "She asks for Tinuke. Tinuke will not see her."

The chief spoke to Shoye. He said: "Why do you wait here?"

Shoye answered: "I have a friend in my village. She borrowed my beauty. She came here. She now lives in your house. She does not return to her village. She does not return what she borrowed."

The chief said: "You mean that beautiful girl that I have taken as my wife? How could such beauty not belong to the one who wears it?" He sent for Tinuke. She came. She saw Shoye. She was ashamed. She gave Shoye's beauty back to her. Shoye took it. Her face shone. She walked gracefully. Tinuke was now ugly.

People said: "Whenever has a chief had so ugly a wife?"

The chief said: "Beauty and good character are not the same thing. Because a woman wears beauty does not mean that she behaves well. This girl Tinuke came to me wearing beauty, but her character was faulty. Shoye, who was ugly because someone else borrowed her beauty, her behavior was good. One may borrow beauty but not good character. Thus, beauty deceives. And, therefore, I order that henceforth one may not lend his beauty to another. Each person shall wear what is his own."

Thereafter, it was this way. One could neither lend nor borrow beauty. Each person wore what was his own. And there came to be a saying:

"Beauty is only worn; it is not the same as character."

Notes on the Stories

THE stories in this collection are mostly from the Yoruba people of Western Nigeria, but several tales from the neighboring Ibo and Hausa are included. Many Yoruba animal tales are known elsewhere. The animal trickster hero (or villain) who appears in countless Yoruba stories—Ijapa the tortoise—plays a role in Yoruba lore that is almost identical to that of Anansi the spider among the Ashanti and to that of the hare in other regions of West Africa. Like Anansi, Ijapa is shrewd (sometimes even wise), conniving, greedy, indolent, unreliable, ambitious, exhibitionistic, unpredictable, aggressive, generally preposterous, and sometimes stupid. Though he has a bad character, his tricks, if ingenious enough, can excite admiration. Though he may be the victor in a contest of wits, his success does not teach that bad behavior is justifiable. He exists as a projection of evil forces and bad behavior against which mankind must contend, sometimes winning, sometimes losing. Ijapa himself dies many deaths. While many of his adventures parallel those of

127

other West African tricksters, quite a few seem to be localized among the Yoruba. Ijapa has survived in United States Negro folklore as Brother Terrapin.

In the Yoruba setting, Ijapa is something more than an actor in tales of conflict. He is alluded to in songs (some of which may have come from tales), in sayings, and in proverbs. He is used as a kind of yardstick against which human behavior, human foibles, and moral strength are measured. One proverb associated with Ijapa appears in the front of this book:

> Ijapa said: "It emerges!"
> His son cried out: "I seize it!"
> Ijapa asked: "What did you seize?"
> His son asked: "What did you say had emerged?"

(A ridiculous statement elicits another ridiculous statement; a ridiculous question elicits a ridiculous answer.)

Here are some other examples of Ijapa proverbs:

If Ijapa is rich in medicine, why can't he cure himself?

(Said of a boastful person who seems helpless when he himself is in difficulty. "Physician, heal thyself.")

"Practice makes perfect," says Ijapa.

(Identical to our own saying.)

Though Ijapa has no legs on the ground, he has wisdom in his head.

(A person who is deficient in one quality may be strong in another.)

128

As this collection suggests, there is a wide variety of Yoruba tales other than those featuring animal characters. A large category of tales is called *itan* (legend) and deals with events that are considered to have actually occurred or that might or might not have occurred. If not believed, they are at least accepted in the fashion we accept some Biblical tales. Were the story of Noah's Ark a part of the Yoruba literature, it would be referred to as *itan*.

Some of the tales about humans (other than legends) belong to a widespread African repertory. A good many of them, like the animal tales, have counterparts in regions quite distant from Nigeria. There are some obvious intrusions from the Islamic culture area, stretching from Northern Nigeria through North Africa to the Middle East and beyond. A number of Yoruba stories are known in similar or diverse forms in Europe and Asia.

Magic (or "medicine"), supernatural events, and various types of spirits and demons abound in Yoruba lore. The use of magic powders or jujus (articles prepared by cult priests to give special powers to those who wear them) is a commonplace element in dramatic conflicts, which sometimes are essentially a struggle between magic forces. God and the traditional *orisha* (deities of the Yoruba pantheon) sometimes appear as characters in tales as well as in the myths. Yoruba oral literature contains its share of what some of us would characterize as gruesome themes, though a close look at European tales suggests that the Yoruba tradition is not alone in this respect.

Yoruba legends and creation myths have a uniqueness that is not characteristic of the common folk tale, particu-

129

larly as they relate to the ancient and sacred town of Ife. Ife is considered the place where things began. It was the first town where humans lived, the place from which mankind spread out to populate the world. (The first people, of course, were Yorubas.) Three stories in this collection are Ife myths, and some others, though they do not specifically mention Ife, may have once belonged to the Ife cycle. In its beginnings, Ife was a town shrouded in mystery and innocence, a place that was the handiwork of the gods (or God), where life was good and where people had direct contact with the original forces of the universe. Explanations of how Ife came to be are various and inconsistent, frequently contradictory. One version recorded by A. B. Ellis in the nineteenth century (*The Yoruba-Speaking Peoples of the Slave Coast of West Africa*) says that the first man, Obalofun, and the first woman, Iya, were born of the female deity Yemaja and settled in Ife, beginning the human race. Another story mentioned by Ellis suggests that Ife was founded and settled after a migration from the north. According to this myth, a small party from a more northerly region came into the environs of where Ife now stands and found only water covering the earth. The hero of the migration, called Okambi, dropped a palm nut in the water, and it grew instantly into a tree. The travelers climbed into the tree to rest. Okambi then dropped a little earth in the water. It spread out on all sides and became land. In this way the land of the Yorubas was formed, and Okambi became the first Yoruba king.

What most Ife myths are consistent about is that the

town and its surroundings were a kind of Garden of Eden. Many of the stories have marked religious overtones, for they are, in fact, religious explanations. But for the non-African, the religious quality may be heightened because of seeming parallels with Western religious literature. In the story, "How the People of Ife Became Scattered," for example, there are events that remind us of the fall and eviction of Adam and Eve from the Garden of Eden or of the dispersal of man from the Tower of Babel. In the story, "How Moremi Saved the Town of Ife," the sacrifice of a woman's son to the spirit of a sacred stream recalls the Biblical tale of Abraham and Isaac. Some Christian Yorubas see the sacrifice as a version of the Crucifixion and the Ascension and regard the name Moremi as a Yoruba equivalent of Maria. It is of course possible that some of the Ife motifs were influenced by Christian tradition, but the parallels are often strained, and the Ife stories do not have to be understood in terms other than their own.

The town of Ife exists today. It is generally accepted that the Ifa system of divination, known throughout a large part of Nigeria and in neighboring Dahomey, had its origins in ancient Ife.

Some of these Yoruba tales were taken down from Yoruba informants over a period of years. By far the largest number were collected with the help of Ezekiel A. Eshugbayi of Ilesha, Nigeria, to whom I give warmest thanks. I also want to thank Dr. William Bascom for helping me disentangle some confusions about leopards, Ife, etc.

OLOMU'S BUSH RAT: The comic aspect of this tale—
the hiding of the stolen meat on the chief's head—recalls
an Ashanti tale in which Anansi, the spider trickster, hides
stolen hot beans in his cap and thereby suffers a burnt head.
The song sung by the aggrieved country man is an important element in the story. Voicing complaint or criticism
through songs is a deep-rooted institution in African cultures. An offended person is able to make his case public in
this way and get the attention he might not otherwise be
able to arouse. This explains the hesitancy of the chief and
his friends to punish the country man without a thorough
investigation of the matter. The story indicates that a chief's
behavior is expected to be beyond reproach and that even
a chief must answer for his actions.

THE MAN WHO LOOKED FOR DEATH: The
personification of death is almost universal in folklore. In
one European tale with many variants, a man persuades
Death not to call for him at the appointed time. But as
he grows old and feeble and becomes afflicted with ill-
ness and misery, he finally goes out in search of Death,
to be released from his compact. In one Russian story, a
man who has offended Death is punished by never being
called for. In an American Negro tale, each time Death
comes, an old man sends him away, telling him to come
back later. In the end, the old man never dies, merely
withers away. In this Yoruba story, there is an obvious
irony in Aiye-Gbege's change of heart after Ayo pro-
vides him with temporary relief.

EKUN AND OPOLO GO LOOKING FOR WIVES: Several familiar African folkloric themes are blended together here into a unified whole. The two companions in search of wives recall an Ashanti tale originally collected by W. H. Barker and C. Sinclair. The Ashanti story also has the companions changing clothes, but when they return home, it is finally seen that Nothing (who had been clothed in Anansi's rags) is a man of quality, and the wives choose him over Anansi. In the Yoruba tale, virtue wins over Ekun's tactics because Opolo is a formidable opponent. The sequence of the frog talking from Ekun's belly also has an Ashanti counterpart. (See Herskovits and Herskovits, "Tales in Pidgin English from Ashanti," *Journal of American Folklore*, Vol. 50, No. 195, January-March 1937.) The theme of exchanging outward appearances occurs in another tale in this book, "Why No One Lends His Beauty." Ekun's stratagems and excuses to avoid going into battle recall Eghal Shillet, a pseudo hero in Somali lore.

Among Nigerians the name Ekun is generally translated into English as "tiger." As the true tiger is found only in Asia, it is obvious that the term Ekun refers to another member of the cat family, probably the leopard. This is substantiated by the fact that Nigerians describe the tiger (Ekun) as having spots. One non-Nigerian informant reports that a bronze casting in the Lagos Museum includes the figure of a leopard, which is identified as an *ekun*. Disentangling the confusion is made more difficult, however, by the fact that there is another member of the cat family, also spotted, which the Yoruba identify as a leopard. He is called *amo-tekun* and may be what we know as the cheetah. In Yoruba tradition the leopard is closely identified with kingship, and the Obas are said to regard it as a totem. According to one informant, if a leopard is killed by a hunter, it is brought to the Oba. A complicated ritual ensues in which the Oba takes possession of the leopard. The hunter is first scolded and then rewarded. In describing the ritual, the informant referred to the animal as a "tiger." I am certain that some of my Yoruba friends will be disappointed that Ekun turns out, in this tale, to be the leopard. I probably would feel similarly if an African told me that the creature on which a man rides is really a rabbit, not a horse.

THE LIZARD'S LOST MEAT: Wrestling as a sport is known throughout most of Africa, and in many regions wrestlers—like bards—may have a professional status. They may go from one town to another to meet local challengers. An established "professional" wrestler may travel with a retinue of supporters and assistants, including musicians. If there is a drummer among them, he signals the arrival of the group, beating out tones that constitute praises for his champion. The actual wrestling bout is frequently accompanied by drumming, horn blowing, and singing, the supporters of the contestants cheering their champions on in this manner. If a match takes place to entertain a chief or other important person, he may give gifts to the winner. In other circumstances a town or village may put up a purse. The idea of a woman wrestler (the female hyena) is of course preposterous, and it goads the male hyena into a rash action that he comes to regret. Although the tale is essentially humorous, it does not end without an explanation—why the lizard may be seen in the village and why the hyena avoids it. This is the significance of No-Room-for-Both, the Lizard's praise name (a name reserved for special occasions when a person's actions or accomplishments are praised in a recitative or song).

THE ANTELOPE SKIN: This is the Yoruba version of counting chickens before they are hatched, but it contains social comment as well. There is a somewhat similar Indonesian story about a hunter who finds a sleeping deer in the forest. He hangs his tobacco pouch on the deer's antler while he takes a smoke and dreams of how he will pyramid his captured game into great wealth. The deer wakes up and runs away, taking the hunter's tobacco pouch with him. The Yoruba tale comments indirectly on boasting, suggesting that even someone highly skilled at a particular thing can fail when he least expects it. The action of the deer in running away without his skin is a real surprise element—something even an experienced hunter could never foresee.

OLODE THE HUNTER BECOMES AN OBA: The tragedy of Olode is obviously a morality play. Out of pity the King of the Bush gives him everything that a man might want, with a single condition attached. But good fortune goes to Olode's head. He violates the single

135

condition, because it seems to him that he should be deprived of nothing, and he thus returns to a state of poverty. The tragic concept is almost classical. Being poor is commonplace. But having tasted life as a king makes poverty, when it comes again, very bitter. The theme of the forbidden door is widely dispersed in folklore. It appears in a variety of forms in Africa, Europe, and Asia, and apparent survivals of the African version have been found in New World Negro communities.

HOW IJAPA, WHO WAS SHORT, BECAME LONG: This tale of retribution for an ungenerous action closely resembles a story told in Ghana and Togo, in which the spider trickster is the local offender. Anansi invites the tortoise to eat with him but keeps sending the tortoise back to the spring to wash himself. By the time the tortoise meets the spider's standards of cleanliness, the food is all consumed. In turn, Anansi is invited to eat with the tortoise. The meal is set out under water, and because Anansi is so light, he cannot submerge. He ingeniously fills his jacket pockets with pebbles and thus sinks to the bottom. The tortoise points out that it is impolite to eat with one's jacket on, and when the spider removes his jacket, he immediately floats to the surface. In its various forms this tale stresses the theme of good versus bad behavior and the probability that one bad action may be repaid with another. Although Ijapa is usually an unsympathetic character because of his avarice, in the present story he is seen as the offended party.

IJAPA CRIES FOR HIS HORSE: Ijapa's insatiable greed is fully revealed in this story. Once he finds a formula for getting bounty from the Oba, he cannot restrain himself from working it again and again until, at last, the Oba has had too much. There are many episodes in Ijapa's life that end, as here, in disgrace. A proverb sometimes used when a person behaves in an Ijapa-like manner is this one: "When Ijapa was going on a visit to the house of his in-laws, he was asked, 'When will you return?' He replied, 'When disgrace has stepped in.' "

KIGBO AND THE BUSH SPIRITS: The theme of unleashing a force that subsequently cannot be restrained is encountered often in African lore. There are numerous variants in Africa, for example, of the story of the pot and the whip. Found (or otherwise obtained) by the greedy trickster (spider, hare, or tortoise), the pot gives endless food when properly commanded. When the trickster's friends learn about it, they use it. It annoys him that they are benefiting from the pot, and when he finds a whip at the place where he originally obtained the pot, he invites his friends to give it the magic command. They do so and are beaten, but are unable to give the formula that would cause it to stop. Perhaps one of the best of this genre of tales is the Ashanti story about Anansi and his magic sword. Set into action against an invading army, the sword wipes out the invaders. But Anansi doesn't know the formula for stopping it, so it kills the defending army as well, and eventually Anansi himself. In the

Yoruba tale about Kigbo (whose name signifies "obstinate person"), there is no magical phrase either to begin or end the action. Instead, there is the unshakable determination of the bush spirits to help Kigbo, regardless of what he may be doing. In the background, of course, there is a moral preachment. In most Yoruba variants, the denouement is tragic, reinforcing the moral point. (The bush spirits beat Kigbo and his family to death.) Though this present version is atypical in its ending, it is probably more suitable in this collection. A New World Negro version of the tale is known in Haiti.

THE CHIEF'S KNIFE: This tale has a philosophical tone and makes a self-evident comment on human foibles. Mr. Eshugbayi believes that it is not Yoruba in origin but probably comes from the Mid-Western region of Nigeria.

WHY THE LION, THE VULTURE, AND THE HYENA DO NOT LIVE TOGETHER: Here we have the explanation of two facts of life—why the animals that share the lion's kill are not friendly and why the vulture's head is bald. In African oral literature there are many different accounts of how the vulture came by his bald head, just as there are a variety of explanations for the "cracked" shell of the tortoise. The Yoruba themselves have more than one explanation. The theme of unlike animals living together for a time, only to discover that it will not work, is found throughout Africa, and its counterpart has been recorded among the

Indians of Brazil. The Indian tale recounts how the deer and the jaguar once shared a house and why they no longer do so. Another Yoruba explanation of how the vulture got its bald head is found in the tale, "The Quarrel Between Ile and Orun."

IJAPA AND THE OBA REPAIR A ROOF: The idea of tricking a chief or a king into performing a service he deems to be beneath the dignity of his office is of course universally appealing. In African lore it is frequently the local trickster hero (tortoise, hare, or spider) who accomplishes the act of *lese majesty*. In East African tales of this kind, the responsibility of taking the king down a peg is sometimes assigned to the human trickster Abunuwas, whose prototype was an eighth century Arabic poet by the same name. The proverb with which this Yoruba story ends has been altered slightly to make its meaning more clear. Literally translated from the original, the proverb says: "It is on the same day that someone is sent on errand duty by the Oba that the Oba himself should be sent on errand duty." That is, if one wants to see the Oba at work, it should be accomplished while the work is going on. The proverb is cited as a wise saying of Ijapa. The original story contains some further episodes (in which Ijapa gives the Oba a knock on the head), which are not included here because they seem anticlimactic.

SOFO'S ESCAPE FROM THE LEOPARD: This is a Hausa tale from Northern Nigeria, which is strongly influenced by Islamic tradition. An implicit irony of the tale is that Sofo's father, a religious teacher, appears confident that the charm he made with a quotation from the Koran was instrumental in saving his son from certain death. Charms of this kind are commonplace throughout Islamic North Africa. Some are worn around the neck, some on the arms, some sewn into clothing or encased in the scabbards of knives. Holy men of certain sects are sometimes seen wearing scores or even hundreds of such charms. It should be noted that Sofo's bird hunting is not wanton. Small game is much prized as food. There is special humor for the Hausa in Sofo's quoting a proverb to his learned father when questioned about his sling.

HOW OLOGBON-ORI SOUGHT WISDOM: The story of the traveler and his son who try to please everyone along the route of their journey appears in many places and forms. This Yoruba tale has a certain indefinable Middle Eastern flavor, and the presence of a riding camel suggests that the story may have come down from the Moslem north. In other respects it is quite compatible with sub-Saharan tradition and recalls any number of tales about men going out on quests of various kinds—for example, a story included in this collection, "The Man Who Looked for Death." A tale collected by Melville J. Herskovits in Dahomey tells about a king who goes out into the world to seek poverty. What many of these quests have in common is that the objects being sought are in the nature of abstract concepts. A tale taken down by George Herzog in Liberia has two young men going out into the forest to capture sleep. This Yoruba tale about Ologbon-Ori recalls a Panchatantra story which ends, in the words of the translator, Arthur W. Ryder:

"Scholarship's no substitute for common sense,
Attain, if you can, intelligence. . . ."

IJAPA AND YANRINBO SWEAR AN OATH: Here we have a picture of Ijapa in all his aspects—greedy, dishonest, without concern for others, and extremely clever. Though he emerges as the victor over both the victim of his theft and the trial by ordeal (which of course has the nature of law), this does not imply that his conduct gets moral approval. The Yoruba listener regards Ijapa's behavior as wrong in every detail. Though in this instance crime pays off, justice is merely delayed. In another adventure yet to come, Ijapa is certain to receive well-merited punishment. The image of Ijapa's wife sitting on his shoulders and the meaning of his oath that he did not "stretch up his hand" become more understandable when it is realized that the storage house stands well above the ground level on stilts. Sitting on his shoulders, Yanrinbo merely has to put her hand into the opening, and Ijapa doesn't have to reach up. Trials by ordeal appear frequently in African lore, as in another story in this collection, "Ijapa and the Hot-Water Test."

ANTELOPE'S MOTHER: THE WOMAN IN THE MOON: In one form or another the central theme of this tale—the sacrifice of the mother in time of famine—

is widespread in Africa. In one form there is a compact among the animals that one of the creatures evades through some trick comparable to the antelope's ruse in the Yoruba tale. In another form the local trickster avenges himself against another creature of the bush by getting him to eat, without knowing, a member of his family. It is evident that there are variants outside of Africa also. The logical gap in this Yoruba story—how the antelope transported his mother to the moon in the first place—is apparently not a matter of concern.

THE OBA ASKS FOR A MOUNTAIN: This is an unusual version of the plot in which an impossible request is answered with an impossible reply. Many variants appear throughout Africa. Among the Kru, a person commanded by a king to weave a mat from rice grains asks for an old mat of the same kind to use as a pattern. Among the Bemba, a man commanded to carve a lute out of stone asks that the king give him a carrying pad made of smoke so that he can transport the stone lute to the city. The variations on the idea are virtually numberless.

THE JOURNEY TO LAGOS: Do-Not-Advise-Me is called in Yoruba *Ma-Gba-Mi-Ni'yanju.* Ride-No-One's-Back is called *Mase-Gun-Ehin-Eni-Keni.* In the Yoruba setting, the morals implicit in the story are clear, as is indicated in the closing lines. It is commonplace for one person to carry another who is ill or crippled, but the idea of one person not being able to get off another's back has a comic aspect despite the tragic ending. The incapability of Ride-No-One's-Back to dismount is understood to be the result of a taboo having been violated.

IJAPA GOES TO THE OSANYIN SHRINE: Ijapa's getting the farmer to "punish" him by imprisoning him with the grain is a familiar type of ruse by the animal trickster hero, even though it does not in this case free him. It recalls how the hawk talks his captors into throwing him over a cliff (Ethiopia); how the turtle gets the monkey to throw him into the sea (Philippines); and how the American Brer Rabbit gets himself thrown into the briar patch. Ijapa's scolding his head, neck, legs, etc., is reminiscent of an episode in the life of the Mexican animal trickster hero, coyote, who asks what his ears, eyes, legs, and feet did to help him escape from his pursuers. When he decides that his tail did nothing to help, he pushes it out of his hiding place, and it is seized by the waiting dogs. The Osanyin priest is an oracle or diviner similar to the Ifa oracle among the Yorubas. The tale "explains" how it happened that tortoise meat became sacred to the Osanyin cult.

IJAPA AND THE HOT-WATER TEST: Again, as in "Ijapa and Yanrinbo Swear an Oath," Ijapa here has to undergo a trial by ordeal because of theft. In the previous trial, Ijapa survived by the clever wording of his oath, while in this one he improvises to outwit the assemblage. The story accounts for a proverb, but it also reflects on the miscarriage of justice. The fact that Ijapa triumphs over what is "right" in many adventures projects an African realization that justice is imperfect and sometimes absent. While Western literary tradition demands that justice be done in some fashion, or that evil be accounted for, the African point of view is that good and evil exist as components of life. Sometimes justice wins out, sometimes not. The victory of evil has as many lessons in it as the victory of good. Beyond that fact, however, the African recognizes the existence of whim and amoral forces in nature. The deity Eshu is sometimes personified as the element of whim, accident, and irrationality that surrounds human life.

OGUNGBEMI AND THE BATTLE IN THE BUSH: Here we have another "how it began" story providing explanations for night and day, for why wild vines are always entangled with one another as though in struggle, and for why the ants are always busy crawling on them. Many African stories end in this way, with one thing turning into another, sometimes into plants, sometimes into animals, etc. The inventiveness of the African storyteller who "explains" through tales how commonplace phenomena came to be seems virtually endless. This type of story is far from being exclusively African, however. An Indonesian tale explains the beginning of dolphins, who once were men. A Malaysian story explains why the ground vine crawls on the ground, why maize stands in the open fields, and why the yam sits under the ground. Magic or "medicine" is a frequent element in African stories, and often it is the critical force on which the final outcome depends. In this instance the conflict turns into a stalemate.

THE QUARREL BETWEEN ILE AND ORUN: In the "how it began" genre of tales, a great deal of attention has been given to cosmic phenomena—earth, sky, moon, sun, stars, and so on. This Yoruba account of how earth and sky became separated is one of several known in Western Nigeria. Another explanation is that the lepers insisted on wiping their hands on the sky until, in disgust, the sky raised itself to unreachable heights. It is perhaps noteworthy that in many cultures around the world there is the concept of the earth and sky once having been close together. Among the Maori of New Zealand, for example, it is said that the demigod Maui was responsible for pushing the sky up to its present position. Quarrels such as that between Ile and Orun frequently figure in cosmic explanations. Among the neighboring Ashanti, for example, a quarrel among the deities resulted in the sun (or moon) being where it now is instead of on earth. In Haiti an African-derived tale accounts for the presence of the evening star in the sky. Again in this Yoruba story, we are told how the vulture came to have a bald head. (See "Why the Lion, the Vulture, and the Hyena Do Not Live Together.") As occurs in so many African stories, the action develops out of a drought and famine. These adversities of nature appear to have made a strong impact on African oral literature. Behind the quarrel between Orun and Ife lies the unspoken issue of seniority.

To the African, it is taken for granted that if one portion is larger than another, it should go to the older person.

IJAPA DEMANDS CORN FUFU: Another story based on the idea of abusing a magic formula. (See notes to "Kigbo and the Bush Spirits.") Fufu is a kind of mush that can be made from various roots and vegetables.

THE WRESTLERS: This simple Hausa story takes note of the cat's unique ability to land right side up and explains how the cat came to be a domestic creature. It seems not to be considered incongruous that the lion should succeed in defeating the elephant, that the goat should defeat the lion, and so on, though such happenings would be regarded as impossible in real life.

HOW THE PEOPLE OF IFE BECAME SCATTERED: A Yoruba explanation of how different peoples came to inhabit the earth. As mentioned in the general notes, above, the narrative has elements that suggest Biblical influence or parallels. Ife has something of the character of the Garden of Eden, and the dispersion of the people calls to mind events surrounding the building of the Tower of Babel.

HOW MOREMI SAVED THE TOWN OF IFE: Another story about the sacred town of Ife. As mentioned in the general notes, the sacrifice of the boy recalls the

Old Testament story of Abraham and Isaac, though in the Yoruba myth heavenly intervention comes after the sacrifice rather than before. Some Yoruba informants see in the story a parallel with the Crucifixion of Jesus. Whether Christian influence helped to shape this story or bent an old Yoruba myth into its present form is not at all clear. The details themselves are overwhelmingly African, and though the parallels exist, one may speculate that if the Yoruba myth were merely an adaptation of a Biblical story, there would be more conformity to the original. The idea of sacrificing a son to achieve a social good is found elsewhere in African oral literature. In an Ashanti tale, for example, a woman gives her son as a hostage so that the people can acquire yams from a distant land. Egunguns are known among contemporary Yorubas as "masquerades." In earlier times egunguns were believed to be men risen from the dead. Men dressed in robes made of long grass or raffia appeared in the streets as though they had returned from the land of the dead. It was believed that to touch an egungun meant death. Whenever an egungun was seen, people scattered. Though it was generally known that underneath the costume was a man, the egungun was feared. Ile-Igbo means, literally, town of the Igbos. Moremi is considered by many Yoruba people to be an *orisha* (deity).

THE STAFF OF ORANMIYAN: Oranmiyan, sometimes called Oranyan, is considered the mythological father of the Ife people and hence the "father" of the Yoruba people. He appears in the myths of the ancient

147

cultures of Oyo, Benin, and other cities and is most widely known by the name Shango. It is believed that Oranmiyan, or Shango, was one of the early rulers of Oyo and the founder of Yorubaland and a long line of Yoruba kings. After his death he became deified. As the *orisha* (spirit or god) Shango, he was considered, among other things, as the source of thunder and lightning. Shango cults exist today not only in Nigeria but also in the New World in such places as Haiti, Brazil, Cuba, Trinidad, and other regions where Yoruba people were transplanted during the days of the slave trade. There are frequent references to Oranmiyan, or Shango, in Yoruba oral literature. Some of the myths and legends verge on the historical and no doubt are derived out of tribal history. One of many versions says that Shango left Oyo with one of his wives and, despondent, hanged himself in the forest. The legend that he was not really dead apparently arose almost instantly, and thus true history blended into myth and the supernatural. This story about Oranmiyan's staff is well known among the Yoruba, and various versions of it have appeared in print.

THE FIRST WOMAN TO SAY "DIM": Lurking behind the naïvely stated problem in this Ibo "how it began" story may be a vague allusion to a time when woman did not acknowledge the nature of marriage as it is understood today. In the absence of information about ancient marital relationships, however, it is safer to conclude that the tale is merely one of those countless accounts

devised long after the fact to pin down the beginning
of a phenomenon or institution.

WHY NO ONE LENDS HIS BEAUTY: The frequent
device of masquerading in another person's clothes (as
in "Ekun and Opolo Go Looking for Wives") is here ex-
tended to wearing another person's beauty—his actual
physical features. The story says in effect that such a
thing was once possible and "explains" why it cannot be
done any longer. It goes beyond simple explanation, however, and ends with a philosophical insight.

Glossary and Pronunciation Guide

YORUBA vowels have sounds familiar in the English language. For example:

a is pronounced like the *a* in father (*ah*).
e has long and short values, pronounced *ay* and *eh*.
i is generally pronounced *ee*.
o has long and short values, pronounced *oh* and *aw*.
u is pronounced *oo*, as in book.

The Yoruba consonant combination *gb* has no exact equivalent in English, though it is nearer *b* than *g*. For easy pronunciation, the *g* may be ignored.

Agbo (ah-(g)boh)—an herb drink
Agbonrin (ah-(g)bawn-rin)—deer
Agiri-Asasa (ah-gee-ree-ah-sah-sah)—a man's name
Aiye-Gbege (ah-yay-(g)beh-geh)—a man's name
Aja (ah-jah)—dog
Alangba (ah-lahn-(g)bah)—lizard
Ayo (ah-yoh)—a man's name

Babalawo (bah-bah-lah-woh)—a priest or diviner of the Fa cult

Bamidele (bah-mee-day-lay)—a man's name

Benin (beh-neen or bee-neen)—a city, formerly a kingdom

Dim (deem, vowel slightly shortened)—Ibo language, "my husband"

Dolapo (daw-lah-paw)—a woman's name

Ekun (eh-koon)—leopard

Ekute (ay-koo-teh)—bush rat

Etu (eh-too)—antelope

Ewure (ay-woo-reh)—goat

Fufu (foo-foo)—a mashed food

Gbo ((g)boh)—the name of a village

Hausa (hah-oo-sah)—a people and language of Northern Nigeria

Ibo (ee-boh)—a people and language of Eastern Nigeria

Ife (ee-feh)—a city, more properly a town, in Nigeria

Igun (ee-goon)—vulture

Ijapa (ee-jah-pah)—tortoise

Ikoko (ee-koh-koh)—hyena

Ile (ee-leh)—the earth

Ile-Igbo (ee-lay-ee-(g)boh)—a town

Ilesha (ee-lay-shah)—a city, formerly a kingdom

Kigbo (kee-(g)boh)—a man's name

Kiniun (ki(short *i*)-nee-oon)—lion

Koran (koh-rahn)—Muslim holy book

Lagos (lay-gohss)—the capital city of Nigeria

Maka (mah-kah)—Ibo language, a man's name

Nwayem (nwah-yehm)—Ibo language, "my wife"

Nwokem (nwoh-kehm)—Ibo language, "my friend"

Oba (aw-bah)—king or paramount chief
Odi (oh-dee)—a man's name
Ogungbemi (oh-goon-(g)bay-mee)—a boy's name
Ojalugba (aw-jah-loo-(g)bah)—a man's name
Ojo (oh-joh)—a boy's name
Ojola (oh-joh-lah)—boa
Oke-Umo (oh-kay-oo-moh)—the name of a mountain
Olaiya (aw-lai-yah)—a man's name
Olode (aw-law-deh)—hunter
Ologbon-Ori (aw-law-(g)bawn-oh-ree)—a man's name
Olomu (oh-loh-moo)—a man's name
Oluigbo (oh-loo-ee-(g)boh)—the name of the king of the
  forest
Opolo (aw-paw-law)—frog
Oranmiyan (aw-rahn-mee-yahn)—an ancestor hero of Ife
Orun (aw-roon)—the sky
Osanyin (aw-sahn-yeen)—the name of a Yoruba divin-
  ing cult
Shoye (shoh-yay)—a woman's name
Sofo (soh-foh)—Hausa language, a boy's name
Swahili (swah-hee-lee)—a language widely spoken in East
  Africa
Tinuke (tee-noo-keh or ti(short *i*)-noo-keh)—a woman's
  name
Wasimi (wah-see-mee)—a city
Yanrinbo (yahn-reen-boh)—wife of Ijapa the tortoise
Yoruba (yoh-roo-bah)—the people and language of West-
  ern Nigeria